I0531435

SAVING ADDY

The Farskons – Book One

MEGAN ENGLISH

SAVING ADDY by Megan English

Copyright © Megan English February 2020

ISBN: 978-0-6487872-1-1

Cover Art: Clayton White

Saving Addy by Megan English

When an attack leaves Addy, her young daughter and her best friend floating in space in a tiny life-pod with dwindling supplies, they can only hope someone will find them.

Preferably someone friendly.

Wouldn't it be an odd twist of fate to have the handsome alien ambassador she'd been trading with earlier that day find her?

But ha! That would never happen. Besides she stinks to high heaven and looks like crap. He was on his way home. He'd never find her.

Or would he?

Dedication

For Ashlee, Aj, Nicole and Caitlin.
No more asking for more chapters! It's done!

Chapter 1

Addy nearly sighed in frustration. This meeting was going nowhere fast. She brushed back at a stray blonde curl of hair that had escaped the braid that hung down her spine, back behind her ear.

"Ambassador I'm sorry. We simply can't. I'll put this bluntly. We cannot give you that much in the first segment without damaging our entire planet's ecosystem. We've only just gotten everything back under control after the decades of industrial waste our ancestors built up. To do this now will undermine everything we've achieved." She paused and glanced at the handsome alien's jawline as it clenched, while his eyes glared at her from across the table. Glancing down her Orb Tablet she quickly did some calculations. "What about a third of what you're asking with the following shipments to come every six months instead of yearly?"

Surely he'd go for that? Earth desperately needed to get rid of its carbon pollution but doing so too quickly could have disastrous repercussions. While the planet Farskon was beautiful it also had incredible weapons systems. And Earth, being so new to space travel, really needed to make some powerful friends. Why not make them with those that needed pollution gases to fuel the factories that make incredible weapons? Farskon was ingenious at finding a way to use their pollution for the good of their people, but they'd gotten so good at it, that they'd run out of pollution. Who knew it was even possible?

They'd been in this meeting for hours already while all the other officials went on about ways to get both parties what they needed. All Addy wanted to do was get out of the room as soon as she could. Her large plush diplomat's suite was waiting for her and also a certain little someone. She couldn't wait to hold her baby girl in her arms again. At eight and a half months old Quinn had just started crawling. And god if her proud little smile wasn't the best thing ever. If she could just get this exhaustingly slow meeting moving, she could get back and snuggle with her little girl.

Why had she ever wanted to be a bloody diplomat? She'd never been so bored in her life, even while she studied to be one. Oh that's right- she'd thought it would be romantic to help her people by her husband's side.

Addy shut that thought down real quick. *Fool. Why would you think of that?* No need to add pain to her boredom.

Instead she gave herself a chance to openly study the Farskon's ambassador sitting on the opposite side of the large oval table with five male Farskons flanking him. She'd seen that his hair was held back in a braid that finished somewhere between his shoulder blades as he'd walked into the room followed by his equally as large men. He seemed to hold all positions for his people-negotiator, diplomat, scientist, and military man. She had to admit that with his nearly seven-foot height and the bulk of his shoulders he certainly seemed to be able to take all that weight of responsibility.

His unusually golden eyes flicked their gaze to her right to the stuffy little scientist who was now backing up her claims. Even from this distance of nearly six feet away Addy could tell there was something almost mercurial about his eyes. The golden gaze matched his deeply bronzed skin. And the long dark lashes would've given him an exotic human look if his bone structure wasn't so prominent. His wide full lips softened the harshness of his face but only marginally. The sharp fangs she sometimes saw as he spoke didn't help either. The male might be a diplomat, but he was definitely an apex predator.

Rix Nahr. A harsh name for a harsh face. And body. Boy, she was sure with the amount of muscle he was carrying he would *definitely* be harsh. Deadly. The tattoos twisting down his arms only made that clearer. They even crossed just below his throat to wrap around the sides of his neck and disappear under his dark coat. She assumed they ran down his back.

Yet another of her colleagues was prattling on now. The large ambassador hadn't gotten a chance to speak in what felt to her like forever. Hardly polite for them to not give him a chance to counter their...what was it now? Fifth offer?

"What are your thoughts Ambassador Rix Nahr?" She said, rudely cutting off the portly man two seats to her right. Not that she cared at this point. It was obvious that h e wanted far more than Earth could or would give. She just wanted to hear that deep rumble of a voice again.

Then those golden eyes fixed on her.

Moments passed and she could've sworn the big male's eyes flashed. With what emotion she wasn't sure. He was incredibly hard to read. She found herself wondering what they'd look like filled with passion. Her skin flushed with heat. Apex predator indeed, what would it be like to be hunted by a male like Rix Narh?

Addy blinked and shifted in her seat uncrossing and recrossing her legs, hoping she disguised her sudden uncomfortableness by adjusting her Orb tablet.

Rix's deep voice interrupted her fidgeting. "No."

"No?" Addy looked up from her Orb, confused. "No what?"

General Jerry Izacks ground his heel down on her toe under the table and shot her a glare from her right. Addy barely flinched.

"What Ambassador Addison means to say is-"

"I know what she meant General. Six monthly half shipments is not enough for the amount of defensive weaponry you are asking for. This is not a fair deal." Another man on Addy's right started to speak but was cut off when Rix raised his hand. "We will leave this meeting as it is. A failure. There are other matters that need my attention but in two weeks' time I will be able to come back to you.

The Setco Defence System your government is wanting is not the only one my people can offer. There are many that will safeguard your people and will cause less of an impact on your planet's fragile ecosystem. I will return in fourteen sleep cycles with some more appropriate offers than I was told to be prepared for."

Those golden eyes burned into the gaze of each of the idiotic men sitting on Addy's side of the table.

Rix Nahr stood and Addy barely smothered a smile. Her government's officials were still gaping from the Farskon's thinly veiled accusations of Earth's greediness. They wanted the most advanced weapons defence system but had obviously talked up their availability of capturing and containing Earth's pollution gases.

Rix and his males were gathering near the door as Addy walked around the table, ignoring the muttering officials around her. She moved quickly and quietly so the other officials didn't notice her. The general, and hell, even her brother would kick her ass later for approaching the largely unknown males of this race alone but she was curious to get near him. Them. Yep them.

Shit, who was she fooling. Him. She wanted to be near *Him*.

She hadn't had this kind of response to a man since she first met her husband. Pain shot through her chest at that thought but she squashed it just as quick as it came. No point dwelling on the past. Her man was gone. Nothing would change that. And hadn't her brother been saying she needed to let go? Move on. Start seeing new people. It'd been over a year now.

But was another race that no one knew much about really who she wanted to rebound on?

Probably not.

But hey at least her lady bits were actually taking notice of someone for a change. Not that she'd been looking. Quinn was more than she'd ever hoped for after losing her husband when the pilot of his shuttle had tried to dock while watching porn. The hull breach had been catastrophic, killing everyone on board. She found out a week later she was pregnant. And she hadn't been sure what was worse. Losing the man she loved or now facing raising his baby alone.

So she'd transferred herself from the smaller shuttle her husband had preferred and been based on by using the payout she'd gotten from his death to get a luxury cabin on the largest space cruiser Earth had had at the time. Which also had the added benefit of having the most government officials on board and she'd been able to speed up her diplomatic trade studies. She'd essentially taken over her late husband's roll as ambassador all before she was three months pregnant. It'd also given her an escape from her grief. Then her maternity leave had started and she'd been in a better head space to grieve properly and deeply. And quickly. She'd worried her brother Alex so much at her apparent quick acceptance of Graham's death that he'd also transferred himself onto the same cruiser, also snagging himself a promotion to Commander. All the better to watch her with. He was now head of security under General Izacks.

Hence the ass kicking.

A large male with deep brown hair noticed her approach. His skin was almost the same shade as Rix's, though his eyes weren't quiet as golden, more a lovely chestnut brown. He tapped Rix's arm alerting him to her presence. All five of the males turned to stare at her. A glance over her shoulder told her no one had noticed her missing as they bickered amongst themselves.

As she got close Addy moved nearer to the male that first noticed her to the left. There was another scary looking male staring at her to the right. His eyes looked black and she saw he had what looked like empty knife sheaths strapped all over his torso. The soldiers must have confiscated them when the Farskons boarded the Cruiser. Addy swallowed around the lump in her throat and spoke quietly to avoid alerting the general. It definitely wasn't because of the tiny niggle of fear slithering down her spine now that she was so close to them.

"Ambassador Rix Nahr, I wanted to thank you for being honest and calling the general and the others out on their shit." She paused, unsure if he'd take offence to her swearing. Nothing. "We do need defences and you need our carbon gases to make that happen. If the six-monthly shipments are truly not quite enough I can get our people started on them straight away anyway to at least move the process along when you get back in two weekly cycles."

A dark eyebrow rose over one golden eye. "You knew they wanted too much for what could be given?"

"No. I apologise. I was also given the impression we could afford that defence system, but we obviously cannot. Yet. I'll get to work on that myself. Although I must say, on earth our men have a reputation for being greedy and assuming that anyone different to them is less intelligent." She tried not to glance at the General. She really did.

She decided to be utterly blunt. "Those that are unlucky enough to be born without a penis and breasts instead have to work twice as hard to be taken seriously."

That earned her a couple of quiet growls from behind Rix. "Your males do not appreciate the intelligence of their females?"

"Not always no."

"Then how do they know they are their female's right choice?"

"They don't. And tend to get pissy about it. There are some that don't have that problem. I was lucky enough to find one who appreciated me."

Another growl. This time from Rix himself. Interesting.

"You have a male?" Hmm was the attraction mutual?

Maybe she had a hope after all.

"Did. He died a year ago."

Rix's features softened. "You lost your male?"

She risked another glance at the far side of the table. "Yes. Look I don't have much time before the General realises I'm over here unaccompanied. Don't let them fool you if I'm not at the next meeting. We need this. Desperately. I probably shouldn't tell you that, but those fools need to stop playing with our people's lives. The quicker this is settled the quicker we're safe. Make them move their asses along."

The corners of his mouth twitched and Rix nodded. "I understand. We need this too. I will heed your advice."

"Thank you. I must go. This meeting has run long enough as it is." She met the gazes of the other dark males behind Rix before nodding her head. She met Rix Nahr's golden eyes. "Thank you for coming today. It was my great pleasure. You're the first alien race I've met and I've gotta say. I'm not disappointed."

And with that she winked and quickly walked away, smiling as she heard a choked sound come behind her. She didn't dare look over her shoulder to see who it came from as she reached the door and walked through.

§

Addy had made it halfway down the corridor to the lifts before she heard someone shout her name.

"Ambassador Addison!"

She stopped and turned to see General Izacks storming towards her with the rather portly scientist Richard Willers struggling to keep up with him. Both men were scowling.

Shit. They must've seen her talking to the Farskons.

"Addison! If you hadn't have opened your damn mouth we'd still be in there negotiating! We nearly had them!" Richard wheezed a little as he reached her.

"No we didn't." She held up a hand to stop what she sure was going to be huffed insults about her having a vagina. "You and I both know that was a colossal failure. You asked for the highest rated weapons system they had didn't you?" She looked at both of them, saw she was right and continued before they could. "You idiots! What you should've done was ask for something medium. Something that could defend Earth adequately while we started trading. Waited for a few successful trades and then asked to upgrade what we already had!" She balled her fists to avoid poking them in their soft squashy chests. "Now we're two weeks behind and we still don't have a defence system capable of taking out a small asteroid let alone a bloody battleship! I swear you lot are the greediest most self-centred assholes that could possibly have represented earth!"

Addy spun on her heel and continued down the corridor to the lifts. Her daughter was waiting for her, and the quicker she left the better. She gasped when her arm was painfully wrapped in a tight grip and she was yanked around again. She tripped and hit the wall with her shoulder.

"Now listen here you hoity toity little bitch!" General Izacks' face had gone an odd shade of red in his rage. "You've been at this gig for what? Two months!? You watch your smart mouth-"

"Gerry..." Richard looked surprised at the rage the general was showing.

"Stay out of this Dick." He tightened his grip on Addy's arm, hard. "I know you paid your way here with your dead husband's money so don't think for a second that you know more than I do. I've been in space since-"

"Since when? Since before I was sucking on my mama's titty?! Don't be so clichéd General." Addy barely kept her anger in check but when a deep snarl sounded from behind the general, she seized the moment to grab his wrist with her other hand, stomp hard on his foot, twist and bring her knee up into his groin. She'd probably pay for that later but dammit she was an Ambassador for shit's sake! Man handling her in front of a witness, a piss poor one, but a witness non the less was an offence. General or not.

Izacks shouted in pain and hunched over releasing her arm instantly and holding his crotch. He glared at her but Richard and her both ignored him, starring over him at the source of the snarling and growling.

Rix Nahr snarled again, clashing those sharp fangs as he bent and grabbed the groaning general by the upper arm, hauling him up.

"You dare touch a female that way?!" His voice came out in a barely understandable growl. "Even for your people she is small. And holds a position of respect!" He snarled again making the generals' red face become sickly pale as he finally realised his situation. "I demand to speak with another of your males." He leaned down into the generals' face. "One of honour, with an understanding of proper respect. I'll not deal with a rikstarg slug like you." Rix roughly dropped the general looking around at the small crowd that had gathered expectantly. "Well?"

An aid and three officials ran down the hall to the lifts while another went to the coms in the corner. Two of the Farskon males bent and held the general upright as he continued to moan and cradle his crotch.

Addy righted her pants and uniform jacket and was about to move further down the hall a bit when a gentle handheld her shoulder. Looking up she saw Rix looking at her arm. The general's grip had been so tight it wrinkled her jacket sleeve. She met his gaze again before he said something to one of his males behind him.

"Valco, come assess the ambassador's arm please." The male with the deep brown hair moved to her side.

She was still starring into Rix's eyes when the male cleared his throat. "Would you please remove the outer layer of clothing? Valco is a medic and has been studying human's medical information. He can see if your arm is injured."

"Oh. Right." Addy looked at her arm and started to remove her uniform jacket. "I'm sure it's just a bruise. I'll have a worse bump on my shoulder from the wall I'd guess."

Rix's features tightened in anger again as he let out a vicious snarl. "You hit the wall?!"

Addy shrugged out of her uniform jacket and checked herself out. "I'm fine, look. Just a bruise around my arm. Nothing else." Rix's reaction to her being hurt confused her but then he did seem to hold females in high regard.

He suddenly stepped into her space, standing so close that if he breathed too deeply her breasts would touch his abdomen. His fingers lightly touched the angry red marks on her arm. He growled again. Addy was starting to like the growling. She lightly placed a hand on his chest in front of her and had to bend her neck to look up into his face. He head didn't quite reach his shoulders.

Then as suddenly as he was there, he was gone again, stepping back out of her reach and motioning the one called Valco forward.

Switching her focus to the Farskon medic she noticed his eyes also had the odd swirling effect his leader's had, although not as golden. His features were also just as harsh, if a little bit lighter in skin tone and hair.

The medic carefully inspected her arm and then her shoulder. He never looked at her eyes but was gentle. He didn't look very impressed though. Maybe the female respect thing was cultural and not just limited to the ambassador?

Valco stepped back and quietly addressed Rix before moving further away to stand with the others of his kind.

"Look I'm fine. There's somewhere else I'm eager to be." Addy looked at Richard. "Can you handle this?

The little man spluttered for a second.

"Sorry Addy. You need to stay and sort this mess out. I saw

enough from the conference room doorway, but we need to hear your account." Another official, Senator Markus Kane, stepped forward. He was one of the more reasonable voices amongst the officials sent to represent Earth in their trade deal with the Farskons. He turned addressing Rix. "This won't take a moment as most of us saw the appalling behaviour of the general."

"You need to find a better male for your military. That one is unstable and dishonourable."

Senator Markus nodded in agreement.

General Izacks opened his mouth to argue but was quickly silenced by a shake from the two large Farskons restraining him.

"We will be. You have my word, Ambassador Ward. Please, if you would follow my aid back to the conference room, I'll request my brother Commander General Julias Kane brought here. We thought General Izacks would be alright for this but have been deeply embarrassed by his behavior." The senator shot a glare at the disgraced general. "This is far from over, General. The corridor surveillance tapes would be damning enough without us having overheard your insolence. You've gravely overstepped your bounds." Markus glanced at the security officers that had arrived from the lifts. "Take the general here to the brig and watch him. Activate your body so know everything will be recorded. This man is being court marshalled."

The Farskons lifted the general off his feet and carried him to the lifts as he began to shout obscenities. "You have no authority! I'm a General of the Earth Starfleet Airforce! You're just a piece of shit senator! You can't do anything to me! Officers! I order you to unhand me! Senator! You dick! I'll have your job for this!"

The lift doors opened again and a man in Earth military uniform stepped out followed by more officers.

"I know you didn't just call my little brother a dick Izacks. You're in enough shit without verbally abusing a Senator." The Commander General glared at the man now held by his officers before blowing out a breath and racking his hand through his greying hair. "What a bloody mess. Do as my brother said. This man's career is over. If he tries to bribe you, I'll know." He motioned to the small camera sewn into the officers uniforms before watching them board the lift and the doors close.

"Everyone that saw this happen please convene in Conference Room 4. Ambassador Addison, this includes you. Richard, I know you were unhappy with her but at least you're not a complete prick. Accompany her. I've been monitoring this mess from the Main Control Room." As people started to move to the room across the corridor from the one they'd all just left, Addy's way was blocked by a big hard body.

Julias continued walking and paused by her side addressing the male in front of her. "If you could follow me Ambassador Rix Nahr, I reviewed *all* of your weapons systems and happen to agree with Ms. Addison about only needing a medium level system. But we'll discuss this in further in the conference room. I know you're probably eager to leave but this won't take long now. Damnit, I detest political bullshit." He glanced between Addy and Rix, an eyebrow arching before he cleared his throat. "I'll, ah. Right." He shook his head as he continued to the room, nodding to the other five Farskon as he passed. They followed after a grunt from Rix.

Addy blew out a breath she didn't know she'd been holding and looked back up at Rix. His golden eyes were swirling but his face was otherwise unreadable. "I, um, have to go give a statement it seems."

"Why are you not disappointed in my kind?" His voice seemed deeper than it had in the meeting.

"What? Oh. Ah, I always thought this job would be much more interesting than it has been. But now that I've met my first aliens, I'm glad to say that you are anything but boring."

"Your job is dull?" He frowned.

Addy wanted to take a step back so she could think clearly but found she couldn't move. "There's not a lot of alien races that want to deal with us just yet, so I've been a glorified political aid for the past two months since I finished my studies."

"I think I see. You were hoping to be interacting with more races and being more productive than you have been, yes? Maybe after this you will get, how do your people say it? Action?"

She laughed. "Yes. I've always been impatient, wanting to get into the thick of things as soon as possible. Which was why I was thoroughly sick of the back and forth that was going nowhere in that meeting."

"I appreciate that. My people would rather, get into the thick of it as well." His lips twitched. "I like the way you speak. Much like your Commander General. Blunt. I understand that better. Even if I don't understand the slang." His gaze moved to her hair. "Your colouring is unusual." He wrapped a curl around his finger. "Our women do not have this yellow hair or blue eyes."

"Oh. I ah. My mother was blonde, we call this blonde hair, and my father had my blue eyes. My brother got the blue eyes but has my father's dark hair. I'm think it comes from the Norse people of Northern Europe. On Earth. It's a genetic thing. You probably got that. I'm going to shut up now." God she couldn't think. She hoped he liked her hair and it wasn't offensive to him. He was so dark, she guessed all his people were dark and not just the six of them she'd seen so far.

He grinned at her babbling and she forgot to breathe. It changed the entire look of his face. His hand was still tangled in her hair and she slowly raised hers to his chest again, feeling the warmth of him.

"Addy! What the hell is going on?!"

Rix abruptly dropped his hand and looked over her shoulder as her brother came charging down the corridor from the lift. She'd know that shout anywhere. Rix lowered his voice. "Your brother looks like you but for the dark hair. Next time we trade with your people I will request your presence. You haven't disappointed me either Ambassador Addy."

Addy sucked in a breath when he used her nickname with her title and stood frozen as she watched him look up and grin at her brother before turning and striding back to the conference room and closing the door behind him.

"Addison! Answer me! What is going on? Why was the alien ambassador pawing at your hair?" Alex reached her and she flinched when his hand landed on her bruised arm. "You're hurt! He hurt you?! I'll kill him. I don't care how big he is!"

"No!" She grabbed his shirt to stop him from running off down the hallway. "I'm fine! He didn't hurt me. General Izacks did." She used her hand to force her brother to look at her. "I'm fine. The commander general saw it all on the cameras. It's dealt with. Ambassador Rix Narh defended me and had his medic check my arm. I'm fine." She repeated.

"So what, he was pawing your hair to make sure your arm was ok?" Her brother sarcastic tone made her anger flare.

"No. I said his medic checked my arm. He was touching my hair as his people don't have blonde hair and he was curious! Jesus. You'd think he molested me or something." She pushed her brother away not so gently. "And FYI maybe it wouldn't have been so bad if he did molest me."

The blood drained out of her brother's face "WHAT?"

"Shut up you moron! Bloody hell. I was kidding. Kind of. Oh shut up, don't start yelling again. I've got to give my statement to the officers in CR4. You can find out exactly what happened then. It's basically nothing." She turned, leaving Alex to follow her down the corridor. "It's only because the ambassador and his men saw it all that it's all gotten blown out of proportion. No one wants to make a bad impression with our first alien traders and abusing a woman in front of them will certainly do that. Don't bust a valve. I don't even have to look at you to know you're about to blow." She grinned to herself. "Come on. I want this over with. It's been three hours since I saw my Quinnie. I want this bullshit over with. I need cuddles."

Chapter 2

It had been another 2 hours before Addy finally got back to her cabin door. She fidgeted waiting for her best friend, also her daughter's nanny, to verify it was her through the monitors.

The other conference room was empty, but the time shed been allowed to leave and she was sorry she'd missed Rix Narh before he and his males had left. She hoped he'd keep his word and request for her to be at the next meeting.

The door slid open silently and Addy almost squealed in delight as she saw her little girl's gummy grin as she clumsily crawled toward the door. She bent and scooped her daughter up, making her giggle, and pressed a smacking kiss to her cheeks. Nothing would ever smell as good as her Quinnie's baby fuzz hair.

Except maybe a certain large male. But that was for later when she was alone. In bed. Hmmm.

She bounced her daughter on her hip and smiled at her best friend. "How was she?" Stella brushed her long red hair back over her shoulder as she straightened from picking up various toys off the floor. "Great. She's always great. You know that. She guzzled her bottles like there was no tomorrow and had her nap. We both only just woke up again a few minutes before you called to say you were on your way back. Sorry I'm exhausted. I was hoping to get the place cleaned back up again before you came back but someone," She ruffled Quinn's hair. "Someone thought it would be super helpful to do a number three and explode poop all out the sides of her nappy. I only just finished cleaning that mess up. I mean I know what she eats but damn! What the hell does she eat?!"

Addy laughed and lifted her daughter over her head like a baby fighter jet. "Did you do a pooplosion? Did you? Of course, you did my little shtinky." She twirled and made them both laugh.

Looking back at Stella, Addy clicked her tongue. "Stella, stop. You're fine. Babies make mess. Stop stressing about it. This is your home too. And of course, you can sleep when Quinn does. We both know how exhausting a little person can be. C'mon I'll get us repli-meals and I'll tell you all about the Farskons." She waggled her eyebrows at her friend as she passed.

"Ooh do tell. Are they hot?"

"You have no idea."

ᦞ

Addy and Stella, jolted from the holographic they were watching when a sudden booming started on cabin door.

"What the-"

She quickly ran to check the monitor before it started again and woke Quinn. Alex was outside looking panicked. She quickly let him in.

"Alex what is going on? Are you ok?"

He glanced down the corridor. "Grab your shit and Quinn. You've got a minute Stella. Get what you can. The baby bag and a bag of nappies, nothing else, forget it. MOVE! Addy grab some clothes, not much, stuff you both can wear. Move, move, move, don't question me."

His blank almost military tone scared the shit out of her, and she quickly did as she was told. Alex also grabbed a few things. She noticed from the corner of her eye it was their family related stuff. A hologram of their parents, and one of Stella's family. A couple of toys off the floor and a satchel to shove it all in.

"We've got to move, follow me and stay on my ass. Ignore everything else. Forget everyone else but us. Do you understand me? The alarms are going to start soon." He moved to the door as Stella came from Quinns room carrying the bleary-eyed child wrapped in her little pink blanket. Her face was tight with worry. The fact that she wasn't teasing Alex showed she also felt the tension coming off him.

"What do you mean alarms?" she said.

"Scravers."

Addy went utterly cold and stumbled a bit. Scravers were a cannibalistic race that had been exposed to too much radiation. Savage and without mercy.

She glanced at Stella's pale face and they ran a little faster behind her brother as they hurried down the corridor toward the suites even more expensive than hers. She clutched the bags she held tighter.

"What?! No that can't be!"

"It can. Move your ass girls."

Addy felt sick. How many people were about to die?

"For once I'm glad you wasted Graham's money on that suite. The president isn't on board and that means her escape pod is free. All the other high ranking officials are already on the brig or in the control rooms and are too stupid to have noticed the markings are slightly off on the ship that just docked." He spoke as he jogged down the twisting corridor towards the presidential suite. "I saw but it was too late to warn anyone. They were already releasing the seal locks. I beat feet to get here as fast as I could. If they couldn't notice that shit, then fuck them. You guys are more important than my job."

They came up to the blast doors before the president's private quarters and he placed his hand on the identi-pad. They slid open with a hiss. "Quickly, quickly." As they rushed through the doors and entered the plush cabin, he drew his blaster and shot the control pad, effectively locking them inside.

"Over to the left of the sitting area. The life pods are over there. I'll put you three in the presidential one." Stella gave Quinn back to Addy and found the disguised control pads and opened the pods. Alex joined them opening another pod. "Yours has a cloaking function that will keep you off the Scravers' radar. It's made for two people, but Quinn should be fine. She eats little bits of your meals anyways. And I saw you grab a box of her repli-milk satchels. It's going to be tight for space for a couple days till the distress beacon activates but Stella could hack it and get it going quicker I'm sure if you need to." Alex took their bags and loaded them into the pod. He gave Stella a quick hard hug before turning to Addy. Tears welled in her eyes at the look on her brother's face. Her fear doubled when she realised he didn't think he was going to survive.

"No." She pushed at him when he tried to embrace her. "No! You can squeeze in with us! Please!"

Alex roughly dragged her into his arms, but he was careful not to crush Quinn. "The oxygen would run out too quickly. It's ok baby sis. I'll be right behind you in the other pod." He smiled tightly and a forced a wink. "I'll have all the room in the world. Mine is made for four."

Tears started to fall. "But it doesn't have a cloaking system does it?" Addy choked on a sob. They'd be able to find his pod floating defenceless in space if they happened to look at their radar. Which was a basic thing that they'd always do. Of course they'd find him.

She rushed him and squeezed him as tight as she could with one arm.

"If we get away now surely you'd be able to make it far enough away for them to not worry about you once they're done with the ship-if our people don't stop them first." She had little hope. Scravers were vicious. But maybe their love of killing would keep them occupied long enough for her brother to maybe make it back to Earth. They were only eight sleep cycles away. He had a slim chance. Slim. But one none the less.

They took a moment to look at each other despite the need to rush. Alex spoke first. "I love you Addison. Be strong for this beautiful little girl. Make sure she's strong and knows how to punch properly." His eyes were glassy as he gently cupped his niece's cheek. He bent and gave her a loving kiss to the forehead as her little pudgy hand reached up and played with the stubble on his chin. She gurgled at him and he swallowed hard, trying to hold back his emotion. He coughed and cleared his throat. "Go. You have to get in now."

Addy carefully maneuvered her and Quinn into the small life pod. She starred back out as her brother began to shut the shuttle door. "I love you Alexander. You're the best brother a girl could ever have. Be safe." The door shut on her last words and she buried her head in Quinn's little body and cried. Stella's arms came around her and they both cried together.

How long were they going to be stuck in here?

⁶♦

Rix Nahr tried to keep his anger in check and paced his shuttle's bridge. They'd gotten the distress signal barely five hours after they'd left Earth's space cruiser. His crew had immediately turned around before he'd even been notified. He'd been pacing around behind his pilot ever since.

Craith had demanded to pilot the shuttle, knowing Rix's emotions were unstable. His males had known immediately of his fascination with the human female, however it appeared the small ambassador had also made an impression on his males. Her fighting back against her attacker was admirable.

A growl rippled up Rix's throat when he remembered the marks left on her arms from that incompetent general. Attacking one so much smaller than himself was dishonourable let alone attacking a female. Three of them had voiced a desire to beat on the stupid human.

He'd been unable to stop thinking of Addy even as they'd left the cruiser. He'd liked the sound of her voice. And her scent. He snarled at the memory of her sweet scent. It had grown stronger when she'd been studying him thinking that his attention was on the males talking at him. Then she'd tried to mask her reaction to him by fidgeting with her Orb. He smiled. He was sure the other humans in the room hadn't noticed but all of his males had.

There had been no mistaking how her scent had gotten stronger. The way the lovely pale skin of her face had flushed. He changed the gait of his steps trying to shift himself as his pants got tighter. He was sure her skin would get that pink colour if he got her under him.

He growled again and earned a glare from the pilot in front of him. "If all you're going to do is growl in my ear and wear holes in the floor maybe growling at Bran would be better? At least he'll growl back at you. I can't go any faster, you know this."

"I know this. Apologies." He sighed.

"The Female Ambassador had strength for one so small. All of us saw that. And we liked her for it Rix. We'll discover the cause of the distress call, although the cruiser is still not answering my coms."

Frustration surged again. "What could be stopping them from answering? They're a large vessel. With many people. Someone should be answering."

Craith hit the coms again. "But slow moving and with little defences. They're close to their planet but not entirely safe. We should be able to see them in a few moments."

Rix resumed his pacing while he waited and smothered the urge to growl again. After what felt like hours, he looked out the front of his shuttle and felt the blood leave his face.

"T'urock." Craith swore in their native language, immediately hitting the coms for the rest of the shuttle. "Scravers have attacked the Earth cruiser. Weapons and battle armour immediately. All bodies ready for battle." The sounds of deep snarls and cursing came down the corridors.

The damage to the ship left no argument that his assessment had been wrong. It was standard of Scraver attacks.

Craith looked back at Rix. "How many were on board that cruiser when we left?" "Just under two thousand. Fuck. This is going to be a mess." He bent over the controls looking further out at the cruiser. "Scanning the ship for life forms. It's been hours. There could be no one left."

There was debris floating about the cruiser as it hung slightly off angle in dead space. The stability controls had been damaged, along with the hull of the ship. He could see at least five blast holes on this side alone. Multiple human bodies and some life pods hung in space amongst pieces of the ship, all heavily damaged.

His males gathered behind him. "This is going to take days." One muttered and there were murmurs of agreement.

"I'll contact my father and send coms to Earth directly. Stay on alert in case the Scravers are still in the area. Scan all pods for survivors. Check everything. We don't know what desperate Earthers might've done to try and hide. Craith, send out these coordinates as a known Scraver sighting."

Rix turned, not wanting to look at the destruction before him. He held Valcor's shoulder. "Try and find the female if you can, her ambassador status as might've put her in the higher-ranking cabins."

"Yes Captain. Craith and I will assess any survivors as we go." Rix nodded, thinking the chances of that weren't high.

He left, confident that his males would organise themselves.

Chapter 3

Quinn snored softly as she slept cuddled in Addy's arms while Addy and Stella dozed. The three of them had been stuck in the presidential pod for nearly five sleep cycles now and both her and Stella had long gotten used to their stench. Their food was running low and there were only two of Quinn's milk satchels left. They'd begun rationing themselves yesterday morning.

The plush pod was just big enough for one of the women to stand at a time to stretch tired muscles or rock Quinn to sleep. They had just enough water for one of them to be able to wash themselves tomorrow maybe before they'd have to reserve it for drinking only.

It was their oxygen that worried Addy the most. They had maybe two days left- if they tried to sleep as much as possible from now on.

She refused to think of her brother or the cruiser. Addy didn't have the energy to spare on that while they were stuck in here. It only caused her pain and made her breathing quicken, wasting precious oxygen.

She and Stella had agreed on the second day to not speak anymore instead communicating silently with hand signals and their lifelong friendship of understanding one another's way of thinking.

Stella had also given her old computer programming skills an update and hacked into the pods coms to activate the tracking beacon earlier than it had been set. She'd also found some fatal flaws in the calculations of how long life could be supported.

That was yesterday.

But their hope of there being someone close by to see the beacon had quickly died as the hours passed. They both also avoided thinking whether the Scravers had returned.

There was a dull boom from outside the pod and they looked at one another. Both arched an eyebrow.

Another boom came and this time it sounded close outside. Addy gently placed her daughter down behind her and slid closer to Stella, effectively hiding the infant from the view of the pod's door. They both turned to look at the doors, reaching for each other's hand.

Please let whoever is out there be friendly. Addy thought desperately.

The pod groaned as it was picked up by a docking port, the air locks hissing as they took place and pressurised.

The door opened and Addy blinked a couple of times at the sudden fresh air that came rushing in. She clutched at Stella's hand tighter and looked out.

Standing just outside the door was a very shocked looking Rix Nahr.

Her breath blew out in a massive sigh of relief at them being found by someone friendly to them. And then it sunk in that was indeed Rix Nahr.

Fuuuuccckk. Of course it was *him* that opened the bloody door to her and Stella's five-day freshness. Not to mention the sizable mountain of used nappies they'd studiously ignored.

Growls came from behind him and Addy noticed another six or so males armed to the teeth were gathered in the docking bay. A couple of faces she knew, two she did not. Some had covered their noses.

Oh god. Kill me now.

Stella cleared her throat, making both Addy and Rix jump. "Well as much as this little staring contest is captivating I can see by some of your noses that you can tell I'm fucking desperate for a decent wash in what I hope is a shower unit larger than this tin can of a pod." Stella's voice was husky from lack of use but she turned and winked at Addy, squeezed her hand and promptly reached out her left expectantly. She appeared to assess the gathered males. "Could one of you delicious looking beef cakes possibly help a girl out?"

A male suddenly shoved a still starring Rix out of the way and cupped Stella's hand. Addy recognised him as the medic who had checked on her arm. Valco? She thought that was his name.

"Careful Valco. She bites." Addy's voice was barely above a whisper but she smiled at his shocked expression.

"Shh." Stella shot a glare back at her. "Don't ruin a girl's fun." She looked back at Valco and grinned as she looked him up and down, no doubt taking in the amount of hard muscle.

"Not too hard handsome. Valco was it? Addy down there told me all about how you cared for her bruised arm. For the past few days I've been getting these aches in my legs, for the life of me I have no idea why. Being stuck in a pod surely wouldn't do that. But anyway, I'm sure a simple massage w-" Stella's voice carried on down the docking bay, but Addy stopped listening as her friend made up for being forced to stay quiet for the last half a week. She was sure poor Valco's ears would be ringing within minutes and he'd regret being so eager to get Stella out of the pod.

Instead she focused back on Rix who was still starring at her.

"Hi."

At least her voice was stronger this time.

Slowly as if trying not to spook her, he reached into the pod and offered his hand palm up. She ignored it however and turned around to gather the few bags she and Stella had packed with them. Rix immediately took them, handing them back behind him to another of the males, saying a few things in what she assumed was his native tongue. Addy gently scooped up her still sleeping Quinnie, pressing a light kiss to the little girl's head.

Rix was reaching back in for her when he froze, his gaze locked on Quinn.

The youngling's hair was the exact colour of Addy's. He instinctively knew she was the baby's mother. But he couldn't make himself move.

Not only had Addy managed to survive but she'd also saved her offspring and another human woman with yet another set of hair and eye colours he'd never seen before, firey orange and green.

It was incredible.

He forced himself to step into the small space. He glanced from the tiny sleeping face to Addy's now wary gaze. He was silently proud of the fact that she wasn't blindly trusting him near her offspring despite the attraction that had sparked between them. Smart female. Not that he posed a threat.

He arched a brow at her and moved his hand slightly. Addy gave a sight nod but kept watching him.

Rix looked back down and tenderly touched a pale-yellow curl. By what looked to be a flower-like pattern on the full body suit the youngling wore, he assumed the it was female. He wondered if she'd inherited her mother's blue eyes as well as her yellow curly hair. He spoke quietly so he didn't wake her.

"She's beautiful, Addison." He met her gaze, hoping she'd see his words as truth. After everything she'd been through, he wanted to make sure she knew she was safe now. "Every male on this ship will protect her with his life."

Addy's blue eyes searched his for a moment before she nodded once. "Thank you." She said roughly. "Did you find any other survivors?" She tried to keep the hope for her brother out of her voice.

His expression shuttered and he gestured for her to follow him out of the pod. "We'll speak of that later. Once you have cleaned and eaten something real."

As his large body cleared the door his males got a proper look at Addy, and the small youngling she cradled against her chest, their eyes going wide with shock. They all quickly backed up to make it easier for her to disembark the pod. One looked at Rix and immediately took off at his nod.

Addy's head whipped around to look at him.

"Do not be alarmed. Bran is going to find a suitable cabin for you and your daughter. We only scanned two life forms on the pod." he stepped closer to her but kept his voice low. "Our people revere younglings. Birthings are hard on our females and youngling deaths are many. Your daughter will never be harmed on my ship. Ever." He grinned suddenly. "She may however be completely ... spoilt?" A few of the males chuckled quietly and nodded. They still seemed in awe.

Ralli stepped forward, and Rix tensed. The male's almost black eyes met Addy's.

"Those of us that saw you during the trade meeting admired your strength for a female so small. We respect you." He looked down at the soft snore that came from her arms and actually smiled. "May I ask her name?"

Rix had rarely ever seen the formidable male smile and usually that was while fighting. Ralli was terrifying on a good day. Right now he almost looked tender. And from the looks on the males around him they were as equally as shocked at this new side of him.

Addy, however, genuinely smiled and walked straight up to the male, seemingly unaware of the reactions around her. She bent her neck to look up at his face far above her own.

"You're one intimidating male. But if you can smile at her like that than I'd want a mean one like you standing by her side. My brother's last wish was to keep his niece safe and to make sure she knows how to hit a man properly. I'm assuming you can help with both of those things." She looked down at her daughter's face before gently holding her out for Ralli to hold while everyone in the docking bay stood stunned- Ralli most of all, an expression of awe on his face. He awkwardly held his arms out and Addy helped position the little girl among the weapons strapped to his chest. She brushed a little curl out of the way of her eyes.

Addy looked back up at Ralli. "Her name is Quinn."

Rix and two others lunged forward to stabilise the male as the colour drained out his face. He fought for control of his face as he choked on his breath. "Quinn?" He rasped as he looked back down at the youngling. The look of pure pain etched on his face sent a jolt through her.

Addy's alarmed gazed met Rix's. "Ralli lost his twin brother as a youngling. His name was-"

"Quinn." Addy's eyes teared up and she suddenly hugged Ralli. "God I'm so sorry Ralli. What are the chances?" He hung his head and touched his forehead to the little curls.

"Brother, I wish you'd seen this day." His voice was so low Rix barely heard it.

There were more than a few grunts from the males around him. Ralli raised his head and looked around fiercely. "If anyone makes her cry know I'll make you pay." Hi voice was quiet and deadly.

"Fuck Ralli, no one will be game enough to breathe around her now."

Addy's grin was pure evil when she looked to the male who'd spoken. "Exactly."

Rix barked out a laugh before he could stop it and immediately regretted it when Ralli's black gaze slid to him as Quinn stirred in his arms. But the child merely shifted and snuggled in deeper against the male's chest.

"Come. Bran will have gotten a cabin prepared by now. Ralli and I will take you. The rest of you, you know what to do."

Addy continued to grin and winked at Ralli as they followed Rix.

The Farskon shuttle was larger than Addy was expecting. And it appeared Rix Nahr was not only an Ambassador but Captain of his men or males, as well.

The cabin she and Quinn had been given was large with an open sitting and eating area containing a comfy looking couch and a small in-built table with two stools. There was a separate space at the back for sleeping that she could shut off with sliding doors. A shower unit and closet were to the side of the sleeping area. And for some reason she

immediately loved it.

The one called Bran had found a large crate from the cargo hold, cleaned it and filled it with blankets and pillows for Quinn. It looked like a super chunky cot. She was surprised by his quick thinking and was grateful to not have to share the bed with Quinn. As much as she loved her daughter the little girl could sure kick and twist in her sleep.

She quickly showered herself and Quinn once the baby woke when, despite Ralli's best efforts, she'd jostled when he'd tried to place her in the makeshift cot.

She'd apologised to all three males for how she and Quinn must smell, only to have all three wave it off. Bran had mentioned that three males would've smelled far worse after five days in a tiny pod together- and that he'd know.

Quickly checking herself in the mirror of the closet, Addy rolled the sleeves up once more on the baggy shirt she'd been given. It'd have to make do. She hadn't worried about the pants- even with the drawstring in them they'd swamped her frame. She would just have to wait till the few clothes she'd packed could be washed and returned to her.

"C'mon Quinnie. Time to face facts." She said, looking at her daughter's reflection in the mirror as dread settled into her stomach. Rix had carefully sidestepped her question earlier but she needed to know just how bad it was.

She bent and scooped up her daughter.

There had to be more survivors than just the three of them. Surely.

Chapter 4

After managing to find her way through the unfamiliar ship Addy hesitated at the door to the bridge. Sometimes ignorance really was bliss. She paused and kissed her daughter's soft curls.

"Okay Bub. I can do this."

She stepped onto the bridge where her gaze was immediately drawn to the wrecked ship floating in front of Rix's shuttle. The air froze in her lungs while her body went numb. Somehow, she made it to the controls and pressed against them as she leaned toward the horror before her.

There were multiple blast holes in the side of the cruiser. Debris floated lazily everywhere. Damaged life pods and pieces of unrecognisable bits of metal hung beside charred clothing and human belongings. Recycling units moved methodically throughout the mess, slowly erasing it from memory. But even after five sleep cycles there was still a daunting amount left.

Addy realised there were other shuttles behind the cruiser including the president's personal family shuttle and three military battle stations. She hoped the battle stations were there for their state-of-the-art medical wings and not because they thought there was still a threat from the Scravers.

A gentle hand came around her waist and she took comfort from Stella. Her friend caressed Quinn's cheek when the baby let out a sound of delight at Stella's attention.

"Hi beautiful girl." Stella's hand squeezed Addy's hip. "They only found thirty-four survivors. They'd hidden themselves in the vents and engine compartments." Emotion

filled her soft voice as they both looked out the portal. Only thirty-four from nearly two thousand. Grief struck at the thought of never again seeing faces she'd seen almost every day for the past year.

The women turned at the sound of boots behind them. Rix, and two males entered, their expressions grim. Rix spoke first.

"My shuttle was the first to get here as we'd barely left this quadrant. Your government was exceedingly slow to respond." He scowled as his rage showed. "They thought the distress beacon was a malfunction and waited nearly five hours before responding. By that time only the crew that had barricaded themselves in the control rooms were left. Some civilians had hidden in vents and three crew in engine bay compartments. The rest of the crew, high ranking officials and civilians were gone."

Ralli spoke next. "Your leaders failed in their responsibilities to their own people." He snarled and shook his head apparently unwilling to speak further as his gaze flicked outside. "What a waste of life."

Addy looked out too and couldn't help but agree. How could anyone think a distress beacon was a malfunction? Rage started to boil inside her.

But she needed one more fact.

"Did any of you enter the presidential suite?" Clothing rustled as the males came closer to watch the cleanup efforts outside. Addy passed Quinn into Stella's arms and faced the males.

They nodded. "The blast doors had been locked and the control pads shot out from the inside. Is that the shuttle you took?" Rix watched her carefully but only saw sadness and grief in her eyes.

"Yes. My brother saw the Scravers dock but knew it was too late to warn anyone. Apparently, no one else had noticed that their ship didn't look right. He rushed to warn us and used his security clearance to get us into the presidential suite. He put us in the main pod and said he'd be right behind us in the staff pod. Please tell me he didn't lie and stay behind?" She looked at each face in turn, but they gave nothing away.

"He took the other life pod. He did not stay." He paused and her stomach dropped to her feet.

"They found him didn't they." She whispered unable to look away from Rix's eyes.

"Not quite." He sighed and raked a hand over his hair. "They found him but didn't seem to bother with his pod. But it looks as though the pod's life support system malfunctioned. He's not dead." He quickly added when she sucked in a ragged breath. "But his oxygen levels were dangerously low, and the medics don't know for how long. They have him isolated within a battle station; I was assured he had the best medical team possible."

Addy didn't know what to think. She was relieved he was alive but was he ever going to wake? "Which one?"

"The Revenger."

Ralli snorted. "Appropriate name for a battle station." He got a shove from the male beside him. "'What? It's true!" Addy ignored them, still focused on Rix.

"Do you know if he's going to be in trouble when he wakes? I'm assuming he broke some pretty big rules by putting us in the president's private pod." Stella spoke while swaying Quinn.

Rix's golden eyes locked on her and he paused before answering. "From what I understand no. Your leaders aren't happy with him but after reviewing the cameras on the cruiser they know that even if he'd tried to save anyone else you all would've died. You, Addy and Quinn were the only residents of the executive suites on that floor at the time. All high-ranking people were in the eating cafeterias celebrating our successful trade deal. They were all killed." He looked back at Addy. "Your brother was smart putting you in the cloaked pod."

Rix looked back out to the cruiser and seemed to think for a moment. "I was told if you had survived, your president was going to strip you of your ambassador status." He clasped his hands behind his back still not looking at her.

Addy was shocked but understood. They'd essentially stolen

the president's pod – a personal one belonging to her family, not just the government issue. Stripping her of her status was a fair punishment.

"Can you take me to the President's shuttle?"

He looked at her. "You wish to talk to your leader?"

"Yes. I need to know what kind of punishment my family and I are going to face." Rix appeared shocked. "Punishment?"

"We basically stole a pod."

"To save not only your life but that of your youngling and family!"

"It was still theft."

Now he appeared angry. "You're not being punished Addy. You're one of a few humans that hold a high rank and has experience in space - and with my race. Your leader wanted to make you a senator, if they ever found you."

"What?!"

"Are you serious?!"

Her gasp was smothered by Stella's elated shout. Addy stumbled as her friend playfully shoved her shoulder. "A fucking senator! Holy crap Addy!" She spun in a circle making Quinn laugh and squeal. "You hear that, baby girl! Your Mummy is gonna be the first space based female senator of Earth!"

Addy was still standing in shock. It was all so much to take in. The carnage of the cruiser. Her brother's survival but comatose state. And now she was probably going to be a senator. Her mind was reeling. The implications of this were crazy.

"Holy fuck." She whispered watching as Stella was still twirling with a giggling Quinn. "This is a lot to take in all at once." So many emotions swamped her that she went oddly numb. Again.

"Maybe we should have something to eat before going to the president. I'm going to have to gather my thoughts and work out what the hell is going to happen to my life now." She stopped

Stella's spinning. "Can you take Quinn for me?"

"Of course! Silly question, Add! I'm her Nanny but I'm your best friend first and foremost. You need to get that head of yours working again after we basically slept for a week. Clear those thoughts out. I might be a computer programmer by trade, but I'd happily take that over your political bullshit any day." She gave a smacking kiss to Quinn's soft cheek, earning a huge gummy grin. "Ralli and friend, please show us to the cafeteria."

Ralli looked longingly at Quinn before raising his hands a bit, but he stopped the action. "May I hold her again? She's awake this time." He paused, "You're holding her differently from before."

Stella grinned. "Of course, big man. Here." She passed the curly haired girl over and chuckled at him when Quinn surprised Ralli by holding her hands out to him. She gurgled happily at him when he settled her on his hip the same way Stella had been holding her. A little hand reached up and grabbed a fistful of black hair behind his slightly pointed ear, then tugged sharply. Ralli yelped and gently untangled the little fingers from his hair. He frowned down at Quinn, but his lips twitched as he murmured.

"She's like her mother. A lot of strength in one so small."

The male behind Ralli snorted and smiled at Quinn when she looked him. He spoke to Stella. "I am Craith. Come, we'll show you to our eating area." He chuckled again when Ralli cursed and untangled Quinn's other hand from his hair as they left the bridge room.

It left Addy and her swirling emotions alone with Rix as they both starred out the portal.

"Is being a Senator not a good thing? You friend seemed more pleased than you." Rix's deep voice broke the silence a few moments later.

Addy sighed and played with her hair. "Yes. No. Maybe." She threw her hands up before resting them on the control panel in front of her. "Fuck I don't know. I never really planned on being anything more than an ambassador."

Rix turned his back to the portal and relaxed against the controls, crossed his arms over his chest as he regarded her. "Why not?"

Addy hung her head and starred at her hands trying to find the right words in her already confused head.

She looked over at the big alien beside her.

"Ok, I need to give some basic history first." She pushed away from the controls and paced, feeling Rix's eyes following her. She didn't look at him for fear of being distracted. His hard, entirely masculine body was intimidating, even when at ease.

"My family is wealthy and my late husband came from a family of politicians – that's how we met. We ran in the same boring circles. Parties with the snobbish, pompous people that run my planet. My family always hated my love of swearing, but Graham couldn't care less. He was already a diplomat and wanted to be sent to space to escape his family and, well, the adventure called to him." Rix stayed quiet, simply watching her as she walked and talked so she kept going.

"I fell head over heels for him. Hard and fast kind of thing. And soon we were married and both in space on a government shuttle. I started my training because I was won over by the romance of the idea of us both representing our people and bringing new and wonderful things from other races to our world. Me and him together. And then he died." She shook her head in anger.

"His shuttle pilot was a fool and wasn't paying proper attention when he tried to dock their shuttle and ripped half the docking bay apart on both the shuttle and the space station. Killed himself, my husband and seven others. The fucking idiot was jacking off and watching porn!" She shot a glare at Rix when he growled. "Who does that?" She kept pacing.

"Then two weeks later I start getting sick every bloody

morning and I thought 'oh no. I've got broken hearts syndrome.'"
She glanced up again but thankfully Rix was still quiet. He'd
shifted a bit otherwise not said a word. Though she could tell he
had questions, he let her talk.

"I didn't believe medi-droid when it told me I was pregnant
with Quinn. I made it do the tests three times. By now I was a half-
trained diplomat, alone in space and four weeks pregnant. Within a
week my mother and Stella were out here. My mother is a force to
be reckoned with, and Stella - well Stella, is just plain fierce. She's a
prodigy at programming computers and to top it off the daughter
of one of the three head engineers for Earth's space fleet. If she
wants to go somewhere, no one dares say no. My mother just uses
her money and charm to get people to do whatever she wants. A
donation here and a fundraiser there and ta-dah! Mum has what
she wants.

"Between the two of them, my husbands will was handled, his
money now mine, my training was sped up and I was a newly
instated assistant to Earth's space ambassador with three months
left before my maternity leave started and four months until I was
due to give birth. I bought an executive suite on the Earth Cruiser
big enough for me and Quinn and I was set.

"Then Stella offered to stay and be Quinn's nanny full time.
She was bored with the computer programming, said it was too
easy, and wanted an excuse to stay near me. I couldn't say no."

Addy stopped pacing on the far side of the room from Rix.
"I've only been working as ambassador for two months since my
predecessor retired. So no, at this point I have no ambitions to
become anything more. I'd gotten to where I wanted to be. My
work hours are great, and I actually get to see Quinn and Stella all
the time. If I become a senator, I could be called away for who
knows how long to who knows where. They never stay in one spot
for long." She gestured out at the wrecked cruiser. "At least as
ambassador I stayed on there and simply had to meet you and

whatever other ambassadors were meant to come there. You came to me. I rarely if ever would've had to leave the cruiser. It had a small school that Quinn could've attended and if Stella ever got the itch to program again the Cruiser would've kept her more than busy."

Rix's jaw clenched and he stood slowly, stepping toward her. "You've accomplished a lot in a short amount of time." She backed up but he kept coming and boxed her in against the wall forcing her to look up at him as her back hit the metal behind her. Addy kept her hands down by her side as his came up to rest on either side of her shoulders. His smelled lightly of spices she couldn't identify.

God it had been a long time since she was this up close with a man. Male. Shit. Whatever, he smelled good. But how could she be considering this with her life in as big of a mess as the space just outside the portal to her left.

"Pleases keep talking, I like the sound of your voice."

"Talking about what? How my life never seems to stay quiet anymore? Or how I don't know what the hell to do with it?"

&

Her sweet scent had been teasing him since the moment Rix entered the bridge. She was wearing a shirt that was far too big that he and his males wore to work out in. It hung to her knees. He wished it was his.

And now her soft voice was doing things to his stomach. Those blue eyes of hers stared up into his and her mouth hung open slightly. His gaze fell to her lips. They looked soft. Would they taste sweet like her scent?

Human females to him looked soft all over. He ached to find out. Females of his kind were dark like the males and just as hard. But Addy was all pale milk-like skin and pink lips. Was she pink in other places too? So much was unknown about human females.

Rix knew he was attracted to her but were their kinds even compatible that way? "Rix. Look at me."

"I am." His gaze stayed locked onto her lips as the tip of her pink tongue wet them before they pulled back over her flat teeth when she grinned at his answer.

"At my eyes Rix." She chuckled, and he almost growled at the sweet sound. "Stop. Come on. My eyes are up here." Her hand pointed up at her face. "Usually human women have to say that to stop the men looking at their breasts."

He grinned, flashing fangs, when instead of looking into her eyes, he took in the lovely rounded shapes of her breasts hidden beneath the baggy material of a workout shirt. A laughed escaped him when she shoved at his chest and huffed at him. He took a small step back. And finally met her sharp blue gaze. He grinned again at her exasperated expression.

"I'm serious. We need to talk about this," Addy gestured between them. "Can this even work between us? I mean mechanically speaking?" Blood rushed to his groin when she bit her lip and glanced at the front of his pants.

Her scent flared, making him groan and step back into her space again, this time leaving no space between his body and hers.

He lowered himself a little, gripped her hips and shoved her up. She made him groan again when her legs immediately wrapped around his hips as he used his own to pin her against the wall. Her arms settled around his shoulders and her fingers slid into his hair at the base of his neck, getting them tangled in his braid.

Rix lowered his head to nuzzle into her neck, but her hand curled into a fist in his hair and jerked him back. Addy grinned at him when their eyes met.

"From what I can feel I think we can work. But a few questions first." She grinned at him again when he snarled softly.

"What?" He ground out.

"Do you know if we can transmit diseases?"

"No. My kind are immune to your feeble health issues. Yes, we can work. No, I can't get you pregnant. It's not my time yet. Now shut up." He went to lower his head again but she hadn't let go.

Addy's smile was full of mischief. "I thought you liked my voice and wanted me to keep talking?"

He chuckled and grinned back at her. "Talk then."

As soon as she opened her mouth to speak he invaded it. He snarled deep in his throat at the taste of her soft lips. Her tongue met his and her legs tightened around   him as she moaned against his mouth. She was so sweet and soft. He'd known she would be. What he didn't know was if he'd ever get enough of the taste of this little human. He was quickly becoming addicted after just one kiss.

The spices he smelled of were nothing compared to his taste. Addy practically devoured his mouth, then nipped at his lower lip before licking the sting away.

Rix ground his hips into hers and held back a groan. The scent of her arousal made him wish there were no barriers between them.

Careful of his fangs he tore his mouth from hers and kissed and nibbled his way down her soft skin to where her throat met her shoulder. Addy's hand clenched and unclenched in the hair just above his tattoos as her other one slid to his shoulder. He fought the urge to mark her with his fangs, licking her instead.

"She'll like it if you nibble on her ears."

Rix's head snapped up and he snarled as he looked over his shoulder at Stella and Craith in the doorway. She was grinning as she leaned comfortably against the frame but Craith was failing miserably at trying to hold his laughter in at Stella's comment. How long had they been there?

"Shut up Stella!" Addy's voice was full of humour and just a little husky. Rix smiled a little and was glad she wasn't ashamed to be caught with him like this by her friend and one of his males. She tilted her head to look at them both around him. "What do you want?" Still she made no move to get away from him.

Stella chuckled. "We came to see if you both wanted anything fresh to eat. But it appears you already found something." She waggled her eyebrows as Craith doubled over unable to hold back any longer. "I won't ask if you want dessert." She met Rix's eye and winked. The female actually winked at him.

"Get out Craith. Take the female with you." He rumbled. Addy's body shook with laughter against him. Rix sighed as he looked back at her and rested his head against the shoulder he'd been nibbling on.

"We're coming." Addy said to Stella over him.

"I could see that."

Craith roared with laughter from down the corridor as he tried to drag Stella away and Rix couldn't help but chuckle.

"Enough." He moved back a bit and let Addy slide down his front. He didn't miss the way her eyes widened when she met the hard bulge in his pants. He was sorry though when her legs lowered to take her weight again but he stepped back, still holding her gaze as he reached down to adjust himself.

"Come on kids." Stella shout carried to them. "I'm sure Craith has told everyone what we just walked in on."

Rix snarled. "Shit."

Addy just laughed again and walked out ahead of him.

Chapter 5

A couple of hours later Addy lay on the bed in her cabin staring at the ceiling. She'd had a great time eating with Rix and his crew. She'd met all eight of them now. Valco, Ralli and Craith she knew and could recognise easily. The others still confused her. One of them had made her wary at first with his scars and steady silence, but she soon felt comfortable around even him, Bran was name. He'd been the one that had taken off in the docking bay to set up Quinn's crate cot. Pravi, Harthi and Gorven she could remember the names of but still needed to work on which name belonged to which male.

Quinn had been the main centre of attention despite the easygoing teasing both she and Rix had gotten. The Farskons really must adore children. Or at least these males did. Ralli and Bran encouraged as many giggles and smiles out of Quinn as they could get and she lapped it all up. The eight month old soon had all nine males wrapped around her pudgy little fingers.

Rix was right. She was definitely going to be spoilt rotten while they stayed on his shuttle.

The thought of the large tattooed male made Addy rub her thighs together and she quickly rolled to the end of the bed. She checked to make sure Quinn was still asleep, snuggled into the crate cot.

Addy rolled again onto her back.

Holy Christ could Rix *kiss*. She'd lost all coherent thought the moment he'd taken control of her mouth. And boy didn't he take control. She'd forgotten all about his fangs until they scraped oh so gently down the side of her neck.

She'd also have bruises on her hips and ass from his hands but who the fuck cared? She sure didn't. She hadn't been with a man since Graham, never having enough time between her studies or job and then Quinn. But then she hadn't wanted to be with anyone either.

Now?

She was aching just from the thought of what Rix could do with a too short kiss. Imagine if they hadn't been interrupted?

A chime quietly dinged, alerting her to someone outside her door. Addy frowned and glared at the door. Stella's timing was impeccable yet again.

She got up and quietly slid the bedroom doors closed so their talking wouldn't wake Quinn. She didn't bother checking her clothes. Stella had seen her in far worse condition. She activated the door and started talking.

"Cmon Stella, I was half asleep! What do- oh."

The cabin door opened, showing Rix waiting in the corridor, not Stella. He wore a dark shirt and workout pants. His feet were bare.

Addy tugged at the shirt she wore self-consciously. "You're not Stella."

A dark brow arched, and his lips twitched. "No." Rix paused looking uncertain. "I thought we should talk about what happened on the bridge."

"Oh, uh, sure. Come in."

Addy closed the door behind Rix as he strode into the sitting space. She noticed his long hair was damp and free of its usual braid when he raked a hand through it. He blew out a breath and looked at her.

"I am unsure of where to start. So I'll do as you did and give some background info, as you called it.

"My people take mates. We find ourselves attracted to a female and if she feels the same, our instincts take over and we mate-bond. It usually doesn't take long at all once the attraction starts. We are loyal to our mates until death." He stepped towards her a little. "You are intelligent. You know I'm strongly attracted to you."

Addy blew out the breath she didn't know she'd been holding. "Yes, I had gotten an idea you might be." A smile played on her lips before she grew serious. "I'm guessing your kind don't do casual sex?"

"We do. If the need arises we find another for sex. It's only when there's strong attraction on both sides that we mate-bond."

"Ah. I think I understand. Your instincts somehow know I'm attracted to you, which added with your attraction to me is making them go haywire?"

"Haywire? I do not know this." He frowned.

"Crazy. They're getting confused or uncontrollable?"

"I am not confused. We might have been around each other for a short time, but I already know of your strength and intelligence. You didn't let the grief of losing your first mate stop you from achieving what you wanted and have raised his young alone while also working and representing your people. Your love for your family is strong, as is your sense of justice. You were willing to face an unknown punishment for simply trying to keep yourself and those special to you alive." Rix closed the short distance between them but didn't touch her. "Any male would be honoured to take you as their mate."

Addy searched his gaze and saw nothing but earnest emotion there.

"You're serious. But, but you're right, we've only been around each other for a few hours. And alone twice. For only minutes."

She tried to take a step back but Rix grasped her shoulders, holding her in place.

"I told you it doesn't take long." He spoke as his head lowered, forehead coming down to rest on hers. He closed his eyes and inhaled. "Your scent draws me. It did the moment I sat across from you at the trade deal."

He was crowding her, making her thoughts go cloudy. He said her scent drew him but all she knew was that his was making her lose track of her thoughts. "You smell of spices." She reached up, lightly traced his jaw line and smiled when he leaned into her touch. "Is that your natural scent?"

"Hmm. My senses are much stronger than yours. My kind don't like artificial scents. You smell of a fruit that grows near my home. Creesha Berries." A growl rumbled low in his throat. He opened his eyes again and grinned. "Your scent flared when you were staring at me from across the table that day. It made me hard."

Addy's hand froze against Rix's cheek. "What?"

"Your fidgeting was doing nothing to hide your reaction to your studies of me." He expression turned almost smug. "I liked that reaction."

Addy thought about this for a second. Her eyes widened and she nearly choked, "Your males..."

Rix's smug smile widened. "Yes. They could smell you too." One of his hands moved to the small of her back while the other moved to her hair. She pushed her head agaisnt his hand, liking the feel of it tangled in her hair. His scent was affecting her.

She took a deep breath and shook her head as if to shake off. Frowning she removed herself from his grasp.

"You're not playing fair Rix. What happens if this seduction is successful and we go to bed together? Will you - what is it? Mate me before I've had a chance to fully think about this? It's not just me I have to consider - I have a daughter! I can't seem to think clearly when you're near me," She narrowed her eyes at him, "And you're using that aren't you?" She started to pace around the room.

She felt Rix's golden eyes track her movements. "This walking, does it help when you are stressed?" He didn't deny her veiled accusation of using seduction against her. Instead he sat and made himself comfortable and continued to watch her. She shot a glare at him.

"No. Yes. Kind of. Let me think!"

"Okay." He settled back and sank even more comfortably into the couch, stretched his muscled legs out and crossed his bare feet at the ankles. "I wish to say one more thing."

Addy stopped her pacing and waited.

"Quinn will become mine once we mate-bond." He was certain it would happen. "My family is also wealthy and political, like yours and your deceased mate's. She will never be harmed, Addy, or want for anything. You already know my males would die to protect her. That sentiment will extend from them to my father, brother and cousins."

"Your family would accept a child that isn't even yours? Just like that?" Addy was sceptical. If he was indeed a powerful political figure on Farskon she could see them being upset more than accepting of a child from another planet. "What about your parents?"

"I've said before how birthings are hard on females. My aunt died giving my cousin life. Nixa nearly killed my mother during birth, but our medic was quick and noticed something was wrong. That is exactly how I know my father and Nixa will accept Quinn. Younglings are to be cherished. No matter their race or parentage."

Addy was humbled. If only humans thought that way. "And what of Stella? My brother?"

"They are special to you and therefore will be special to me. Stella, despite her smart mouth, is already. She makes me smile and has brightened the mood of my males immensely. They are cleaning up without my asking in order to impress her with their worthiness. But that choice is hers." He chuckled.

Addy gaped at him. "All of them? They're all attracted to her?" Those poor males, they had no idea what they were in for with Stella.

Rix grinned. "Five are. They made agreements after the two of you left with Quinn earlier that they wouldn't fight one another for her attention. It's simply a competition of their charming skills now. I think your people say 'May the best male win'. They agreed physical fighting around Quinn would not be wise. Nor would angering you or Ralli if they did." His smile died. "Ralli is a former assassin of my father's. The loss of his brother hardened him. You truly couldn't have found a better protector for your daughter. Even if she didn't share his twin's name."

"Honestly I thought he was just dangerous looking with all those knives strapped and covering him. I wasn't really thinking straight but I suppose I instinctively trusted you and your men. So, I figured by picking the most badass one I could find she'd be safe till I knew what was happening." She pointed at him. "You're distracting me again."

Rix grinned and flashed a fang but said nothing. She liked that he wasn't even remotely sorry.

"Would your family hate me?" Addy started pacing again.

"No. They'd only have to be around you for five minutes and they'd see what I do." "Will I be stuck at home making babies for the rest of my life or would I be able to

stay on this ship and still be some sort of ambassador?"

"Mates do not separate for long unless it is by death. I'd slowly whither from not being around you, Addy. If you stayed at my home and I continued to travel space it would eventually kill me." Rix truly looked fearful of the thought of being away from her.

"Wow. Ok."

Minutes passed as Addy continued to pace and try to make sense of the thoughts jumbling through her brain. She was thankful Rix stayed quiet, watching her from the couch and not interrupting.

He studied her face as she moved around the room. Her emotions played out across her features so plainly he could almost predict what she was thinking about.

After a while she stopped and sighed. Her small hands scrubbed her face.

"I don't know what to do." She looked so utterly lost that Rix immediately got up and went to her. She surprised him however, when she turned into his chest, pressing her face into his warmth. She breathed in deeply. "Shit I could get used to those spices of yours. Even if they muddle my brain." He stayed quiet, sensing it was what she still needed and just held her.

"I honestly don't want to be a senator. The workload is far too much and Quinn is so small. I'd never see her, and I don't want to miss the little things as she grows. I wasn't there when she started to crawl. I saw her first steps. But I missed the crawling. What else would I miss if I took that job? She'd probably start calling Stella 'Mum' instead of me."

"Then politely refuse the offer? Your president seemed to be an intelligent female. She'd have to be to want you as one of her senators. She would understand if you explained why." Rix gently pushed and held her away from him to meet her eyes. "I will have to stay near Earth for some time to install the defence system that was traded for. Maybe you could offer to help train some senators and new ambassadors on what to expect when working in space with other races?" He saw her eyes widen and knew she liked that idea. "I'd also be back often, maintaining our trade agreements and working on new ones."

"That would be great! You know you're fairly intelligent yourself." Addy swatted at him playfully. But her smile faded when she looked back up at him. "What? I'm sorry, I was only teasing."

"I could make you happy Addison." He needed her to understand that.

Her head tilted and she regarded him. "I have no doubt about that Rix. I like you. I *really* like you. But we've only kissed once. It was amazing. But it was only the one time." Her hand landed firmly on his chest when he tried to draw her back against him. Her eyes narrowed. "Can we have sex without you mate-bonding t o me?"

He hesitated. "It will be difficult. My instincts are screaming at me to make you mine. But I can try." Rix tried again to get her closer to him.

But Addy resisted him again, pushing at him with her hand. "How does this mate- bonding thing work?"

"I'll bite you during sex. It doesn't hurt. I've been told it can make things more intense. A chemical in my saliva will enter your bloodstream and will change the way you scent. Those spices as you call them will come from you as well. My body will start to want to be near you. Crave you. It can't fully be explained but it has something to do with my scent being on you and pheromones."

"I'm sure they'll be nicer coming from you than me."

"To me you'll still have your sweet scent but mixed with mine." He stepped into her and this time she didn't keep him away.

"I know what you're doing."

He grinned and her resolve melted even more. "It is working though."

"Yes." Her voice sounded husky even to her ears. The hand on his chest slid higher over his shoulder and into his loose hair. "I should tell you, Quinn is asleep. No loud snarls or growls. As much as I like them, I don't want to be interrupted this time."

♠

Rix didn't get a chance to reply before her hand cupped his cheek and she dragged his head down to press her lips to his. Addy's other hand-held his hip as she molded herself to him. They both groaned when he took her invitation and deepened the kiss.

His hands slid down her arms and around to cup her ass as he hoisted her up. He held her easily.

The soft material of her shirt rode up as she wrapped her legs around him. He couldn't help it, a soft snarl tore from his throat when he realised she wore nothing but the shirt. She was bare to him.

He spun and settled them both on the couch. Neither knew whose shirt tore as they stripped.

Tearing himself away from her mouth Rix kissed his way to her breasts. He took a dusty pink tip into his mouth. He loved that she was so soft. His hand kneaded the other breast and she gasped when he lightly nipped her.

"So soft. Everywhere." He murmured before taking his mouth to her other nipple. Addy bit her lip to stop a moan from escaping, her fingers digging into his scalp. She loved the feel of his hands on her. They had a slightly rough texture that rubbed her just right.

Suddenly he raised himself up and slid down her body. Addy made a small sound of protest but Rix needed this. Needed to taste her. He grabbed her feet and shoved them up under her ass spreading her to his view. A low snarl ripped from him at the sight of her sex. He could see how ready she was for him.

His hands slid up to her knees and gently spread them even further before gliding back down to rest on her inner thighs.

An ache settled into her clit at the look of pure hunger on his face as Rix stared at her. He looked half starved. His golden eyes were swirling with passion when he glanced up at her before he scooted back even further, his face hovering so close she could feel his breath fan her.

"You have a little hair here.' He grinned. "I like it."

Addy lost all thought when his mouth firmly latched onto her clit. She arched her back but was unable to escape him. He sucked on her and she had to clamp a hand over to her mouth to muffle her shout. His tongue lapped at her bundle of nerves, moving up and down. His hands on her thighs held her pinned under his face but she couldn't help but buck against his mouth. She moaned again.

She cried out against her hand again when a thick digit entered her. She clenched around it and a snarl came from him. It sent vibrations down his tongue straight to her clit.

She arched as climax hit and panted, unable to make a sound as she rode it out. His tongue never stopped lapping at her, making wave after wave hit.

It took a while for coherent thought to return to Addy as she lay limp. She looked down her body to find Rix's golden eyes watching her. A shudder rippled up her spine when he licked her one last time, his gaze never leaving hers.

Slowly he raised himself and crawled up her body. Addy's eyes widened when she saw his arousal straining toward her. It would seem Rix was impressive all over. She didn't get to dwell on how he was going to fit inside her as he licked and nibbled his way back up her body making her mind go to mush again. Rix pressed a kiss to each of her breasts making her eyes close. His breath blew over one of her dampened nipples and she knew he watched as it pebbled.

"I'll try not to bite you Addy. But I won't lie. The urge to claim you is strong."

"Just give me another day to know you. Please." She whispered before kissing him. Her hands roamed from his face down his shoulders to his chest before wrapping around his back. She curled a leg around his hip and ground herself against his hard length.

Rix was so hard he barely needed to draw his hips back before the head of his cock found her slick entrance. They both moaned as he entered her.

She was so hot and tight around him, she really was soft all over. Rix withdrew and pushed in a little deeper dragging another moan from her. He thrust deeper and deeper until he was seated all the way inside.

He paused, not wanting to move too fast for fear of hurting

her. One hand planted next to her head on the couch, the other clamped on her hip.

"Please." She begged. "Move." Addy's legs tightened around his hips and she thrust her hips up, clenching her inner muscles around his shaft. Her small nails clawed down his back, marking him.

His control snapped and he snarled as he buried his face into her neck, fangs slowly dragging up her throat. He withdrew and thrust his thick cock home again. He moved faster and harder, soon the sound of smacking flesh filling the room.

Addy arched with a silent cry and tightened almost painfully around him before turning her head to his arm, biting down on him as she came.

Rix bit back a snarl and opened his mouth to suck on the soft flesh of her throat. When her soft teeth bit into his forearm again he ripped his head up away from her throat and bit his tongue to keep from roaring out his pleasure. His body went rigid as he came and spilled his seed. His climax rolling through him over and over. Which sent Addy back over the edge, taking her breath away, her muscles twitching around him.

They lay in a heap, tangled together on the couch while Addy's fingertips on his back drew lazy patterns over his skin where she'd marked him earlier. Rix shivered, liking the feel of her touch.

Opening her eyes Addy looked at his arm and saw the neat imprint of her teeth in his tanned skin. She licked his arm to ease the bite mark and pressed a kiss to it.

"You didn't bite me, but I seemed to have bitten you." She murmured.

Raising his head Rix smiled down at her. "I liked it." He shifted and held his weight on his elbows but didn't withdraw from her body. One of his fingers lightly traced along her jaw, down past her ear to play in the stands of her hair. "I'm not sure if I can resist next time."

Her blue eyes met his as she studied him. His hair was a curtain around them. God she'd only been alone with him a matter of hours in total and yet she was totally comfortable with him.

Sliding her hands up his arms she crossed her wrists at the nape of his neck.

"I'm probably crazy for saying this but I'm not entirely sure I want you to resist next time. After that just now," she paused, appearing to search for the right words. "I think you might have ruined me for anyone else."

A soft growl rumbled from Rix as he frowned at her and lowered his head to nip at her nose. "There won't be anyone else!" He kissed her deeply. "*I've* decided it." Addy moaned and he twitched inside her. He was still hard she realised.

"Mmmm. I'm not completely convinced though." She arched a brow at him and bit her lip to keep from smirking at his expression. "You could use a little-"

Rix cut her off with a snarl and pulled out of her. Addy found herself flipped over onto her stomach before she could blink. Warm hands gripped her hips and lifted her before a couple of pillows off the couch was shoved underneath her. The blunt head of him rested at her entrance and she felt his breath fan her ear as he bent over her. His large hands landed on the couch in front of her head.

"You're teasing the wrong male Sweetness." Rix remembered the words Stella had said earlier in the Bridge and nibbled the edge of Addy's ear. Her shudder under him told him it hadn't been a lie. He grinned, what other things would Stella know? He'll have to find out in the future. "But if it's convincing you need, I'm sure I can think of something."

With no more warning than that he thrust back inside her slick channel and made her gasp. Addy threw her head back into his shoulder and bit her lip to keep from crying out. Rix was ruthless as he pounded into her and she loved it.

He hadn't expected her to rock herself back into him, effectively impaling herself deeper and deeper. Rix wasn't sure he'd last much longer. She encased him perfectly, so wet and tight about him. He nibbled along her neck again with just a hint of sharp fang never slowing his hard pace and she stiffened, clamping around him. Unable to control himself he bit down and his fangs pierced her neck.

Addy imploded under him. A rough hand clamped down over her mouth to muffle her scream as spots danced behind her eyes. The burn at her throat was delicious and sent waves of pleasure coursing through her as if a live wire connected her from neck to core. The waves were so intense they sent a second round of release coursing through her before the first has properly finished.

Rix thrust into her once, twice, three times more before she felt him find his release, his hot semen coming in strong spurts she could swear she could feel.

δ♦

They panted together, his fangs and cock both still buried deep inside her. As Rix slowly extracted his teeth from her neck, he kept himself seated in her snug heat. He licked the bite on her neck clean and his saliva quickly sealed it shut keeping traces of him in her veins. He wondered how long it would take for her scent to change.

"Hmm I warned you." He licked her again. "Please tell me you don't regret it." There was a note of vulnerability in his deep voice.

Addy smiled softly into the couch.

"Never. While it might have been a bit fast, I don't think I could ever regret that." Opening her eyes, she turned her head to peer at him over her shoulder. "We'll figure it out. Tomorrow." She looked over the back of the couch to the closed doors and the bedroom that held her sleeping daughter behind it. "For now, I just want to fall asleep in my new mate's arms."

Rix looked at the doors too. He'd not only just gotten a mate but a new daughter too. He smiled at the thought of them all asleep in the same room.

He nuzzled her shoulder one last time and withdrew himself. Snagging her shirt off the floor he gently wiped her clean before handing her his own torn shirt. He didn't care that it was torn but it was his. His mate would only sleep in his clothes now. That or nothing. Quickly cleaning and dressing himself in his loose pants he tossed the shirt toward to the laundry unit.

Addy watched as he stood to his full height and stretched like a cat that had gotten the cream. Then yelped when he scooped her up as if she weighed nothing and strode to the bedroom. She helped open and close the door before Rix gently placed her on the bed.

Her insides melted when he walked to the crate cot and tucked the blankets around Quinn and traced a finger over her cheek. He whispered something in his native language and kissed the sleeping girl.

Then he looked up at Addy and her heart stopped.

"Thank you for giving me not only you but also entrusting me with the care of your beautiful youngling too." The wonder clearly written on his face as he strode to her.

"Oh Rix. How could I not when you clearly love her already?"

He climbed onto the bed with her and lay down between her and the door. He opened his arms and she immediately snuggled down into his side under the covers. His scent enveloped her, and she couldn't stop the sigh that escaped her.

Within moments sleep took them both.

Chapter 6

Addy was warm. Lovely, snuggly warm. She wiggled and snuggled even further into the warmth that surrounded her with a smile.

Smack.

Addy sputtered and opened her eyes and looked at her daughter's smiling little face as she raised a pudgy arm ready to bat at her mother again. A gurgle of happiness told Addy she wouldn't be getting any more sleep.

"That's no way to wake your maram." Rix moved behind Addy, informing her where the warmth had come from. He chuckled when Quinn simply giggled at him. "I didn't get you out of bed so you could attack. Your aim needs some work."

The big male lithely moved over Addy and picked the little baby up. He rolled back onto his back and held her above him to her delight, little legs kicking as she reached down to his face.

"Don't worry little one. I'll teach you all the tricks you may need." Rix had always wanted to play with a youngling this way. He'd never have admitted to another that he was stabbed with jealousy when he saw the mated males of his kind playing with their offspring. He started to make the soft noise of a fighter droid and flew Quinn around as she squealed.

Addy laughed at their antics. Of course, he made fighter droid noises. Males. They were fundamentally the same no matter what planet they came from.

She moved to get out of bed, not worried about her nakedness in front of both her daughter or Rix. After relieving herself in the bathroom she came back to dress but stopped and simply watched.

Mate. She had a mate. Not a husband. She gently rubbed a hand over her throat where Rix had bitten her. A small tingle of awareness spread over her as she touched it. Her lips twitched as the memories of last night flickered through her. An ache settled between her thighs, making her inner muscles clench. Maybe she could convince Stella to give Quinn breakfast? And then she could come and have a morning shower. With Rix.

And now she had an image of a naked Rix covered in water droplets. She licked her lips, wishing she could lick something else.

Quinn squealed and broke her thoughts as Rix now flopped her on the bed and started to tickle her. Not only did Addy have a mate - her daughter had a father again. A very large, super-hot father. Who currently wore a stupid grin as he mercilessly tickled the tiny girl. Addy couldn't help but grin as well.

"Keep doing that and you'll be the one to clean her nappy when she pees herself from laughing too hard."

Rix's head snapped up and his grin slipped when he saw her naked form leaning against the wall of the bathroom unit. His nostrils flared and she knew he could smell her want for him.

Quinn saw an opportunity and made a grab for Rix's hair. He cursed and smiled down at her while Addy chuckled.

"I'm sure I can work out how to clean a tiny human up." He pressed a kissed to her nose before he picked her up and placed her on the floor. She immediately crawled off, heading for the few toys spread on the floor of the sitting area of the cabin.

❦

For a few seconds they both watched at the little padded bottom waggled its way out of the room.

Rix breathed in the heady scent coming from Addy and closed his eyes. Before she could blink he moved and had her in his arms. She gasped and he invaded her mouth. His tongue met hers and she moaned against him.

Their hands roamed, tugging at hair and squeezing ass cheeks.

He grinned and nipped at her before kissing and nibbling his way down the flesh of her throat to her shoulder. He wanted to mark her on this side of her throat as well. Hells, he could think of a lot of places he wanted his mark. He licked her collarbone and growled when her small hand tugged on his hair.

"We've got about two minutes before she comes looking for us or starts to cry." Addy murmured against his jaw.

"Hmm challenge accepted." Rix snarled and gripped her hips. He hoisted her up and she didn't hesitate to lock her thighs around his hips. He pinned her against the wall with a low grunt. The head of his cock bumped against her slick entrance and he didn't wait. He thrust himself deep, gently biting her right shoulder to keep from crying out.

"Fuucck." Addy moaned and clamped herself around the thick cock inside her pussy. She tightened her hold around his shoulders and let him pound up into her. She dropped her head and bit into his shoulder.

A vicious snarl ripped from Rix's throat as her blunt teeth met his skin and increased his pace. Harder and harder he slammed himself inside her. The gentle hold of his teeth increased until he tasted the richness of her blood on his tongue.

Addy became impossibly tight around him and his vision went grey. His movements became uncoordinated and he jerked. His orgasm slammed into the base of his spine and he lost himself in her with a low growl.

The feeling of Rix coming in her sent Addy over the edge as well.

"How long was that?" The smug tone in his voice made her chuckle against him.

Clenching her muscles, she arched a brow as he groaned. "I think I need more data to make a fair comparison."

"I never thought I'd say this, but I think you'll be the death of me little female." Rix sealed the fresh bite mark he'd left on her and softly kissed it. A breath left Addy on a sigh as his kiss sent a tingle through her.

"Is it normal for your mark to make me tingle in my lady parts?"

Rix pulled back, a look of confusion on his face. "Tingle?"

"Ah yeah. Like a feeling down there when you touch or kiss the bite mark. Do your females feel that?"

Rix traced a finger over the mark he left last night, watching her closely.

Addy shuddered and bit her lip to keep from moaning. Her inner muscles twitched as he kept touching the small mostly healed puncture wounds.

A mixed look of surprise and male satisfaction came over him.

"I have not heard of this, no. To us it is simply a mark telling other males that a female is mated and the way for our saliva to change their scent. Interesting that it has this effect on you though." His golden eyes studied her shoulder and then the newer mark. "Is it more intense with the newer bite?"

This time Addy couldn't help the sounds she made as he started to softly prod at the fresh bite. Her muscles tightened and she knew she was perilously close to coming again, just from him touching her bite mark.

Rix lowered his head and licked at her with a grin. Gods she felt good as her pussy pulsed around his hardening cock. What a wonderful surprise from his little human. His grin turned devilish at the thoughts of how he could use this knowledge of his mark on her.

Sucking on the sensitive flesh sent her climax spiralling through her. The heat of her made it hard for hard for him to think as he rocked inside her, drawing it out as long as he could.

"Hmm I think I like this side effect of our races mixing."

"No complaints here either." Addy's voice was husky with satisfaction. Raising his head from her shoulder he kissed her as she came down from the high of her climax.

They grinned at each other when a small wail sounded

from the other room. "Told you."

∂♥

With Quinn playing in the water spray at their feet, Rix and Addy shared a shower. Rix was pulling his pants up when the low ding came from the door. It opened before he had a chance to move.

Stella stared at him from the doorway.

"Holy fuck. Um shit. Although from the look of you I'm sure it was a god like experience. Damn boy!" She grinned and fanned her face in a not entirely mock swoon.

"Stella!"

"What? Girl look at him!" Stella leaned to the side to look behind him at Addy. She pointed at this muscled stomach. "Please tell me you climbed him like a lickable tree!"

Rix chuckled and didn't need to look at Addy to know she'd have a lovely red blush on her cheeks. He finished fastening his pants.

"Stella! Shut up!"

Stella's assessing gaze came back to Rix and she grinned at him. Crossing his arms, he just shrugged and smiled back at her.

"Yup. You did. You *so* did. I can see it on his smug face. And I see he stayed the night too." She chuckled at Addy's huff. "Okay, okay, I'll stop." Rix watched as Stella went to her friend and took a gurgling Quinn into her arms. "The boys wanted me to tell you that breakfast was ready. Although I think Bran is going to have a fun time searching for the Captain here, in the wrong part of the ship." She cooed at Quinn and bopped a tiny nose.

Maybe she could take the little girl and he could have a few minutes alone with Addy while everyone else was at the other end of the ship. They could make all the noise they wanted then.

"Alright, we've just showered and I just need to dress Quinn."

"I can help with that, where are ... Holy shit what is that?!"

Stella's gaze was fixed on the bite mark on Addy's neck.

Rix cleared his throat bringing Stellas now angry gaze to him. "A mating mark." Her green eyes narrowed. "I didn't hurt her, despite what it looks like. Your kind are a bit softer than mine. But I assure you. I'd never hurt her." The corner of his mouth ticked up in a half smile. "Ask Addy about it."

He chuckled as she turned bright red again and nearly groaned aloud when a wave of her scent rolled through the room at him. Unable to stop himself he stalked over to the females. Ignoring Stella, Rix used a finger to tip Addy's chin up and brought her lips to his.

"Mmm. I'll leave you females to your talking. I'll meet you in the cafeteria." He kissed Addy's nose and ruffled the messy little curls of Quinn's head. Winking at a now gaping Stella he left the cabin.

As soon as the door slid closed behind him, he fell back against it and let out a breath he didn't know he'd been holding.

Scrubbing a hand over his face and back through his hair Rix stayed against the door for a while.

Had last night really happened?

"WHAT?!"

He snorted when he heard Stella's shout through the door. Shaking his head, he couldn't wipe the smile off his face as he made his way through the ship to his quarters, easily avoiding Bran when he heard the male's footsteps searching for him.

δ♥

"WHAT?"

Addy winced at Stella's shout. "It's sensitive." She shrugged.

"Woah woah woah. I need to sit down and get this straight." Putting Quinn on the floor with her toys, Stella sat on the couch. "His instincts knew you liked him. And after all of twenty minutes of knowing one another he decided to 'mate' you. Or marry you. Which involves him biting you like a vampire, which then makes your pheromones change and you smell like him. Essentially making you his. And then on top of it all, his bite mark can get you off?" Her friend stared at her in disbelief. Then a look of shrewdness glinted in her eyes. "Can you get yourself off from the bite? Asking for a friend of course." She waved a hand dismissively.

Addy snorted and shook her head. After all of that, of course *that* was what Stella focused on. "Maybe. I don't know. It's just sensitive. Maybe it's more intense when it's him since he's the one that gave it to me?" She sat down next to her friend and watched as her little girl threw her toys about and squealed. "But seriously Stella, you should see him with Quinn." She felt her insides melt at the memory of the two of them playing in bed earlier. "He did the whole lay on his back and make flying noises as he held her up thing."

"Aww!" Stella's face softened. "I must admit all of those big ape men turn to hot muscly goo the moment our girl enters the room. I swear it's the weirdest thing seeing a huge guy covered in deadly weapons coo at a baby girl as if no one else in the room existed. Cute. But weird." She paused for a moment thinking. "I guess this means you won't be Earth's first female senator in space?"

Addy groaned and dropped her head into her hands. "You know I never wanted to be anything more than an ambassador. Being a senator would mean I'd never see Quinn. Or you. The workload is far more than I ever wanted. And way too political. I just wanted to help Earth understand aliens and help smooth over the occasional trade deal. I don't want to get involved with the running of the world or the big decisions on treaties and war. I'll just gather the data needed to help the two sides understand one another."

Stella's arm came around her and she rested her head on her

friends' shoulder. "Quinn isn't walking yet and I don't want to miss her first steps like I did when she started crawling."

"Yeah. I know what you mean. Did I tell you my mother is trying to marry me off to some tech trillionaire?" She sighed. "I don't wanna miss anything either and Quinn isn't even mine. Well, not really." She added when Addy started to protest. "I know you say she's my niece, but my parents don't see that. All they see is ambition and improving one's social status. And even though you're stupid rich you'll never be rich enough for my mother and you're not going to be marrying me or leaving me - her - your fortune in your will. Cold hearted bitch."

Addy couldn't disagree. Stella's mother was something of a monster of a woman. "And we're avoiding the *big* subject. Sooo..." Stella waggled her eyebrows and stuck her tongue between her teeth in an effort to change the subject. "I'm assuming that between the bite mark and sheer size of him that Rix must be pretty skilled in the bedroom?"

Addy grinned but didn't say a word.

"Oh no! No you don't! I want every dirty little detail! Don't you dare skim over it all like you did before! Is he same down there?" Stella waggled her brows with an evil grin.

Chapter 7

Stepping into the cafeteria, Rix stopped as all movement froze. He heard a collective inhale as his males stopped what they were doing and turned to him.

A snicker came from the back of the room and a deep voice broke the silence. "So how many washes did you take to try and hide her scent?"

Rix grinned. "One. And she was with me. I'm not hiding anything." He walked to the back of the room and piled a plate with a small mountain of food. Then grabbed another and piled it with smaller hill for Addy.

"You mated her." Pravi's statement wasn't a question.

"Yes." Would she want a drink to? Maybe he should get a tiny plate for Quinn as well.

A large hand clamped down on his shoulder and spun him around. "So we're compatible with the human females?" Craith stared at him intently.

Rix arched a brow and grinned. "I wouldn't have mated her if we weren't. Besides our medi-pods had already determined that our races were capable of mixing. The only way that could happen is if we, ah, fit."

"But their females are so small." Another voice joined in from the middle of the room.

"We stretch." Stella snickered when all the males but Rix jumped. "Do I need to find a sex ed video and explain the mechanics?"

A round of growls met her statement and she chuckled.

Addy studiously ignored them all and their stares as she made her way to Rix. Her eyes going wide at the sight of the mini food mountain he'd gotten for her. Stella followed her, still grinning.

Ralli approached with a questioning look. Addy grinned when Quinn let out a sound of happiness at him and reached for him before Addy had even made to pass her over. As she turned back toward her food, she flicked her hair over to shoulder and jumped when Ralli let out a snarl, looking at her mark.

He spoke sharply in their native language and more snarls echoed through the room. *"You've marked her harshly Narh."*

Rix stayed quiet. Keeping his eyes on Ralli he came up behind Addy and lowered his head. Slowly he licked over the flushed skin of his mark on her left shoulder from last night and she shuddered. Her scent flared. Rix grinned with pure male pride at her reaction. He answered Ralli in their native tongue. *"Human females bruise easily, but you can see it's not worrying her."*

Ralli's eyes went wide and Stella snickered again.

"Oh yeah. The reaction is totally more intense when it's *him* that does it."

Addy went bright red and quickly whipped her hair back over her shoulder hiding the mark from Ralli and the others as they stood staring at her. She ducked her head and hid a secret smile. She quickly gathered her food and made to move toward a table but found herself boxed in by her big male.

Rix made a point of kissing her in front of collective stares. He grinned again when she looked up at him, her gaze slightly cloudy. Kissing her nose, he stepped out of her way.

Stella chuckled again. "No need to rub, it in big man. We all know you're good." She quickly got herself a meal and joined Addy at a table not far from him.

The other males stared at him or Addy. It was Ralli that found his voice first, the rest still frozen in confusion. "What was that?!"

Rix couldn't help but chuckle. "It seems our matting bites have a small side effect on human females."

"Side effect?"

Stella snorted. "If you touch, kiss, lick, suck on, blow at, nib-"

"Stella."

"Fine. If you are the one to touch the mark *you* made it has an um...arousing effect on the chick. Female. Woman. It can make her come."

"Stella!" Addy practically growled at her from across the table.

"What? It's not like you can deny it! Rix touch her again."

"N-" Addy had to close her eyes as she bit her lip when Rix grazed his thumb on the mark from this morning. He chuckled at the hiss Craith let out and kissed the top of mate's head. "They're just jealous." He whispered to her. He sat beside her and took a mouthful of food without a care in the universe.

"The newer the mark the more intense the reaction." He said between chews.

"Are you sure you didn't mark her too hard Rix?" Ralli was still frowning over by the food dispenser. Quinn wriggled in his arms and played with his hair.

"No." Rix took another huge mouthful of food. "She's just soft and her skin is very responsive to," he paused and grinned a still red Addy who was playing with her food and not yet eating. "Sucking on it. It makes the skin redder is all."

§♥

Please let the floor swallow me up Addy thought as Rix and the *entire* crew discussed her sexual responsiveness as if it were the weather.

A foot nudged her under the table and she looked up at Stella smiling at her.

"They're obviously not shy. You shouldn't be either. Besides I think it's more   curiosity at the difference between us and their females more than anything." She said quietly.

Rix's hand nudged her chin and she looked at him. "I apologise if we embarrassed you but Stella is correct. As I'm sure you guessed, our females don't react the way you do to our bite.

They are as shocked and curious as I was." He smiled at her, the tip of a fang showing. "We are also not shy. I love how responsive you are to me and will take every chance I can to show it. We are an affectionate race. The more affection between a mated couple the stronger the connection. The better the match."

There were a few murmurs of agreement from around the room.

Addy realised they weren't teasing her - they actually were discussing her reactions like the weather. Uncommon and weird weather. Which oddly made her feel a bit better.

"Well, to be fair this has never happened to human women before, so I guess it is a bit odd."

"Odd? Try fucking awesome!" Stella mumbled around a full mouth of food. A snort from one of closer males told Addy that he'd heard her. His smirk also told her he'd love to get the chance to try it on her friend. Even if it was binding and to the death.

Valco moved from his seat near Ralli and approached. Rix paused and narrowed his eyes at the male. Raising his hands Valco paused. "I only wish to inspect the mark and see the effects for myself. I'll add a note into the medical files of her race."

Rix frowned and glanced at Addy. "Wait on adding the note. Once you do her kind and ours will know we've mated. I think she'd rather tell her family herself. As would I."

"Oh. I hadn't thought of that yet. Crap, my parents are going to shit a brick."

A snort sounded from Craith. "Your earth sayings are amusing. Has anyone actually shit a brick? It sounds painful."

"Hence the saying. And no. Well not that I know of." Addy looked at Rix who looked slightly uncomfortable. She patted his leg below the table. "Well they won't freak in a bad way. My mother will be happy. She'll just be surprised that it happened so quickly. And with Alex in a coma it'll be a lot to take in. Maybe we should wait a little bit before announcing it to the collective worlds?"

Rix nodded. "I was actually thinking the same thing."

A male entered and paused. His gaze landed on Rix and Addy as his nostrils flared.

A look of surprise passed over his scarred face as his silver gaze flicked between them. "Your nose doesn't lie Bran. She's mine." Rix's arm came around her possessively.

Bran nodded once and smiled slightly. "Congratulations, Captain." The smile wiped off his face as he continued. "We've received a com from the human's president. They wish to know when the ambassador will be returned to them." His lips twitched in what Addy could only assume was amusement. "Shall I tell them never?"

A few chuckles filled the room. And Addy couldn't help but smile at his deadpan. It seemed the quiet Farskon had a dry sense of humour.

Addy glanced at Rix who nodded at her and continued to eat. She turned back to Bran. "Tell them I'm still recovering from my ordeal and will contact them myself shortly. Also tell them to let my family know I'm not injured. Just wanting to gather my wits before I face the government. Thank you, Bran."

Bran nodded and left without another word.

Rix looked around the room at his males and spoke in the harsh words of his people's language. The males around them nodded and got up and left - all but Ralli who had gotten a plate of finely chopped fruits, stayed with Quinn, helping her choose the choicest morsels.

"I know it's early but we should discuss what you wish to do. You expressed yesterday that you didn't want to be stuck at home making babies and I know how you like your job as ambassador."

Addy nodded and poked her food with her fork thinking.

"If possible I'd like to stay an ambassador." She looked at Rix, his golden eyes doing their swirling thing again. He smiled at her.

"I'm sure between our wealthy families we can arrange

something. You are the first human mated to one of my kind. It would make sense that you stay an ambassador as I am one too."

They grinned at one another.

"Oh for shits sake. Go back to your room. You're grossing me and Ralli out with your cuteness." Stella rolled her eyes and winked at them. "Big man and I can handle Quinnie."

Ralli snorted his agreement. "I can smell you both from over here. Go." Stella looked between Ralli and Addy confused.

"Smell them?"

"The arousal coming from Addy is quite potent."

An evil glint hit Stella's eyes. "Is that so?" She narrowed her eyes at Addy. "Can all of you smell this?"

"Yes. Unfortunately, they can." Addy smiled as she shoved one last mouthful of food in before Rix picked her up and slung her over his shoulder.

"Right, so no checking out the boys when they're close." Stella said nodding, pretending to make notes.

"Our hearing is also exceptional." Ralli's smiled slipped and his eyes narrowed at Rix. "I sleep near your quarters. Keep the roaring to a minimum yes?"

"No promises."

"Roaring?" Stella's head whipped up from her imaginary notebook and she smirked. "Maybe Quinn should move in with me?"

Addy's head popped up over Rix shoulder as he started to leave the room. "Are you offering?!"

"Ha! You wish jellyfish! From the vibes coming off you two someone needs to keep the *mating* to a minimum." Stella waved her fork at the two of them from her seat. "Quinn is just the woman for the job. And I don't even have a Farskon nose."

"But you're her nanny!" Addy mock pouted and Rix snorted. She even got a smirk from Bran and Ralli.

"Oh hurry up and go!"

Rix took off running as Addy's laughter rang out. She kissed his neck making him groan. "My rooms are closer."

ॐ

Hours later Addy shifted nervously on Rix's lap. They'd decided that they would tell his family first via a com and then tell hers in person when they visited her brother tomorrow. Ralli stood at the back of the room with Quinn, out of sight of the com.

"Maybe I shouldn't be sitting on your lap for this." She moved from him and out of view. "I'll come in after you've introduced me."

Rix frowned but didn't get to say anything before the com beeped. He quickly wiped his expression.

After a moment he started talking. Addy wrung her hands and picked at her nails as she listened to him speak. Before long another deep voice came from the com and she assumed he must be speaking with his father. Possibly his mother as well. This was confirmed when a husky but clearly female voice spoke next. Rix smiled at her and spoke again.

After some more back and forth between Rix and his parents he tapped a few things on the coms. Reaching out a hand to her, he spoke in English.

"Addison. Come here and meet my Maram and Preyam. Eleerxi and Froska Nahr." Placing her hand in his, she let him draw her over to him, then yelped when he pulled her into his lap again. She smiled shyly at the couple on the com screen and hoped her hair was ok. "Maram this is Addy, ambassador to Earth."

"Hello." Addy smiled and waved awkwardly.

Both had the sharp, darkly coloured features of their son, although Eleerxi was more of a deep chestnut brown where her mate was a deep midnight black in both eyes and hair. Rix got his golden eyes from his mother, which gave her a shrewd yet not unkind look. Forska however was all dark and terrifying or would have been if it wasn't for the kind expression he wore.

Rix's mother's golden eyes widened when she took in Addy's looks.

"Well. Aren't you striking child!" The com translated her sultry voice into English easily. "I see why he was attracted to you - such exotic colouring. But you are a little

thing."

"Do not underestimate her Maram. She disabled a male almost twice her size when he accosted her."

Forska's kind expression disappeared. "What? Which male did this? There is no honour in attacking one so small!"

"None of your males did, Forska. It was a human male of my kind. A man with little honour and a lot of greed. He did not appreciate a woman pointing out his shortfalls. It is a common thing among human males. Their pride clouds their judgement."

"Your males are fools."

Addy's lips twitched. "I don't disagree but there are a few that can use more than their lower head when thinking."

Eleerxi snorted out a laugh. "I like you, child."

Rix looked over his shoulder at Ralli and nodded.

"There is another person you should meet. This is Quinn." Ralli passed the now dozing baby down to Addy. An audible gasp came from the com, though Addy was unsure who it came from. She adjusted Quinn so that her sleeping face could be easily seen. Rix tucked a little curl away from her face as he continued. "Addy's male was killed in a shuttle accident before either of them knew that little Quinn here existed."

"Her mother's hair colour." whispered Eleerxi. "Does she also have your blue eyes Addison?"

Addy looked up and smiled. "Yes. And I'm worried to think she might also have my attitude - which my mother would say is fair pay back for me as a child."

"Yes. Young are always the mirror of their parents." Eleerxi's golden eyes sparked with amusement at her.

"On Earth we have a word. Karma. What goes around comes around, meaning what you send out will come back to you."

Forska chuckled. "Oh yes. We have something similar. Rix and Nixa have certainly given me my fair share of your karma."

Addy chuckled when Rix grinned, not at all repentant.

Eleerxi cleared her throat. A touch of saddness dimmed the golden light in her eyes. "Rix told us of what happened on your earth cruiser. I'm very sorry for the loss of life your people have sustained."

Addy nodded. "Thank you. I didn't see it thankfully. I can't imagine the horror they faced."

"Indeed." The older female paused. "Rix also told us of your people's leader offering you an even higher position amongst your people. But you do not wish to accept it. May I ask why?"

Addy smiled a little. "Of course, you can. I do not wish to have to such a large workload. Quinn is so small and I have already missed a few of her firsts and I do not wish to miss anymore. My late husband I were meant to share this responsibility but when he died I had not even finished my studies and everything he did fell to me. I had no intention of climbing further up the hierarchy of Earth's politics.

"You already heard how a man didn't take it well when i beat him at his own game. It would only get worse. I like the job I have now. I enjoy it. Being a senator, I would not enjoy."

Eleerxi nodded. "I understand this. Your family comes first, but you still enjoy the amount of work you have now."

"Yes." Addy smiled glad that her … mother? Maram in law? Understood her sentiments.

Eleerxi grinned. "You have strength to not bow to those higher than you simply because it is what they wish. Some would say you are unambitious. But I do not think that is so. You've simply reached where you wanted to be."

Forska nodded. "It would make sense to promote you but I agree with my mate and son. I believe you would be better suited to staying where you are as well. The two of you being ambassadors to your home nations will make things easier for both races."

"Earth needs a few more levelheaded people like you I think." Addy winked. "I've loved meeting you and look forward to doing it again in person. I'm afraid I must go and put this little person in her bed." She nodded to the com and gave Rix a peck on t h e cheek. Helped her off his lap and gave her hip a squeeze.

Returning to his native tongue Rix kept talking with his parents as she left and made her way back through the shuttle to her cabin.

Tucking Quinn in Addy soon collapsed onto the bed.

&♦

Not bothering with the door chime to announce himself, Rix entered Addy's cabin a short time later.

He'd enjoyed talking with his parents. It had been a while since he'd heard their voices. He couldn't say he'd missed the responsibilities he had on their home world however. His parents were practically buried in them. When his father had suggested he become an ambassador for their people and travel the starscape trading and meeting with the other alien races he'd jumped at the chance.

He knew that many of his older relatives looked to him as the next generation, despite the fact there were others able to take on his duties and better suited for the mantle. His cousin for instance. Hell, even his younger brother was a better choice. Both were more even-tempered than him.

He sighed and shook his head. Scrubbing a hand over his face, he decided he'd tell Addy the full extent of his duties and titles back on the home world.

Looking about the cabin he didn't see Addy until he spotted a dark shape on the bed. She was fast asleep. He smiled at her when he heard a soft snore coming from her and decided to check on Quinn.

His smile became an outright grin when he realised both mother and daughter were asleep in the same position, front down on their beds with a leg cocked up. Their hands up near their faces and …what did she call it? Blonde curls a mess around their heads.

Quinn huffed in her sleep and Rix froze. Maybe she needed her little covering. Blanket. He got it and tucked it around her. He heard a tiny sigh come from her and he relaxed.

Leaving Quinn be, he made his way to the main bed and climbed up beside Addy. Tucking her in against him he breathed in her scent. It was starting to mix with his and he smiled.

Who'd have thought a simple trade mission would end up with him finding a mate and an instant family?

Chapter 8

By lunch the next day Addy was exhausted again. She'd spent the morning conversing with all manner of Earth officials via the com on the Bridge, mostly just convincing everyone she was fine. No, the Farskon had not kidnapped her. No, she was not a part of the attack and most definitely had not helped the Scravers on board. No, she didn't want to return to an Earth battleship. Yes, the trade deal had been settled before the attack took place. No, the Farskons were not in the immediate area which was why it took a while for them to arrive to help.

That particular enquiry had made her so angry she'd very nearly snapped at the idiot who'd said it. As if the dickhead thought it had been Rix's responsibility to protect Earth's people even though the cruiser had been within six hours of the planet. She'd had to cut the conversation short, claiming to be overcome with emotion, the poor little feeble female that she was, and needed to rest. She knew the others in the room could tell she was simply outraged at the POS with no brains that had somehow become a Commander General.

Craith had had the good sense to stay quiet once she'd ended the com and hadn't even looked her way as she seethed for a few moments before calming down enough to leave the bridge. Ralli had also taken one look at her when she'd passed him in the corridor and simply let her go. She'd guessed he'd been about to ask where Stella and Quinn were, but she figured he'd find them eventually.

Not wanting to see anyone else, she'd quickly made her way to her rooms.

Now naked and sitting on the floor of the shower unit, Addy didn't want to get up let alone dress and leave the little bubble of Rix's shuttle to meet with the president.

The woman was like a freighter ship. Once she decided something, it happened – and fuck anyone who tried to use politics against her. President Gena Reynolds used their own tactics against them and then out maneuvered them.

Addy just knew this woman had probably figured out she was now involved with Rix and she didn't want to be senator. What she wasn't sure of was how President Gena would use it against her.

On top of it all was the fact that her brother was still comatose. She hadn't really had a chance to think of Alex properly before now. The relief she felt at him being found alive was bittersweet after realising the severity of his condition. No one would know how bad the lack of oxygen had effected him until he woke. Would he have brain damage? Or was there just enough air for him to simply fall asleep and the pod's life support kick in and keep him stable until he was found?

Earth's medics hadn't sent their diagnostic reports on the pod Alex was in, to Rix's shuttle. She figured they must have focused on sending them to her family rather than just her, as bloody frustrating as that was.

Gods she hoped he was ok. Please let him be ok.

Addy looked up as the door chime sounded but lowered her head onto her knees rather than get out. Stella could wait a while. Addy just wanted to wallow for a little.

She realised it wasn't Stella when the door to the shower unit slid open to reveal two large, tanned and very male looking feet.

"Ralli said you were upset but I didn't realise it was this bad." Rix hunkered down but didn't enter the warm spray of water. "Females everywhere it appears like to soak in unbearably hot water."

Addy felt her lips twitch and turned her head but left her temple resting on her knees still. "It's not that hot."

"I can feel my skin melting from here." His voice showed his amusement, but his eyes held a touch of concern. "Craith mentioned you dealt with some intellectually challenged human males this morning. But I suspect your hot water soak means that's not the only thing you're upset about."

Addy closed her eyes for a moment. How he could read her so well already.

"I haven't heard anything more of Alex. Or from my family. And yes, I dealt with some supreme assholes today."

"Assholes?" Rix looked both disgusted and confused, making her chuckle.

"Dick heads. Imbeciles. Wankers. Idiots. Arrogant males that think a woman is only of use when she's flat on her back moaning."

Rix growled. "I think I understand. They insulted you."

"Not directly but they insulted my intelligence by making assumptions - mostly that I'd buy whatever story they had decided they were going to spin to the president. Either that or you and your crew should have stayed until the security system was installed - or that you called the Scravers. Or that I called the Scravers in some act of defiance to show how much we needed the system. Blah blah blah." She waved a hand dismissively and rolled her eyes.

Anger tightened Rix's features. "That's just..."

"Stupid? Infuriating? Yup." She frowned and realised her butt had gone numb from sitting for so long. "I had to get off the com before I blew a valve and lost my ever-loving shit at them."

A low snort reached her from Rix through the falling water. "Ever loving shit." He chuckled, making her smile.

Rix leaned back, staying hunkered down but not bent toward her anymore and her smile slipped as she took in his large form. Only light black pants covered him and his hard torso was bare. The muscles of his legs seemed to be trying to escape. His thighs spread as he balanced on his toes. She noticed there was a draw string at the top of his pants and an idea hit.

Rix was watching her warily as her mood changed. "What? Did I drop some food?"

He looked down at himself and she used his distraction. Her hand shot out and grabbed the drawstring. Yanking with all she had Addy unbalanced her male and he landed hard on his knees at the edge of the spray. Her other hand curled around his nape and she moved her body onto his lap.

"Oh no. Look. Your pants are wet. Looks like you'll have to take them off."

A giggle escaped her at the gutteral groan that ripped from Rix when her wet chest met his.

∂♥

Later the door chimed and slid back to reveal Rix holding Quinn.

"I thought you might want some Quinnie cuddles before we left."

She looked up from her spot on the bed and froze as her breath left her in a rush. Rix was wearing his people's traditional formal outfit. All black leather and a black fabric with a silvery metal as accents in the buttons and fastenings. His arms were bare from the shoulders, all the corded muscle on display. The muted black of his clothing made his black hair shine. Not to mention his golden eyes, she could swear they almost glowed.

They were meant to be having dinner with the president tonight. Just Addy, Rix and two of his males with the president and her husband.

Shit. Now the males were going to know she was hot for her mate the whole time. "You couldn't have worn a sack or something?"

She saw Rix inhale, turning his expression heated. He grinned, showing his sharp teeth. "No."

"Ralli and Valco are going to tease me to no end when they see or smell me."

"They wouldn't dare. Not when I am with you." He winked at her as he passed Quinn into her arms.

She gave her daughter a smacking kiss and played for a few minutes on the bed. "Is Stella coming here?"

"Yes, but I will take Quinnie to Ralli and the rest of the crew. Stella will help you finish dressing. Pravi and Craith have been showing her the traditional dress of our females. The three of them have been modifying it to fit your smaller frame." Rix came to sit on the floor with the two of them. His females. Addy smiled at that.

Wait. Traditional female dress?

"Stella has been doing what with who?"

Rix smiled as he held a toy out to Quinnie. He hadn't called her Quinn since he'd heard Addy use the nickname. Nor had most of the other males for that matter.

"We keep extra traditional outfits on board in case we come into contact with officials from our planet unexpectedly. We won't offend them by accident then. Stella has been modifying one for you." He looked over at Addy. "She mentioned that you didn't pack nice clothes in your haste to leave the cruiser. Obviously. That would've wasted time. But this leaves you without something respectable to wear when meeting with your world leader. And as my mate, it is acceptable for you to wear the dress of my females and not offend my people. Does this not please you?" He studied her as Quinn kept playing.

Addy was stunned. It was thoughtful of not only him but Stella and the two males as well.

"I ... yes, it does." She crawled over to him and pressed a kiss to his lips. "Thank you for thinking of it. I hadn't really thought about my state of dress and would've just apologised and told President Gena that we'd left the cruiser in a hurry." She stroked a finger over his cheek. "But thank you. I'd love to see the traditional dress of your females."

The door to her rooms opened with a chime and Stella strode in like she owned the place, a large amount of black material draped over her arms.

"Geez guys, no fornicating on the carpet. Quinnie doesn't need to see that." She grinned at them and held her arms out. "C'mon woman. This is going to take a little bit and then we're gonna play with your hair. Nothing too fancy, it's not a gala, just an informal formal dinner. But a girls' gotta have some fun every now and again. Rix, chop chop. Grab the baby. The boys have instructions on her care for the next two hours. Out."

"Two hours?!" Addy sputtered.

"Girl, those curls aren't gonna tame themselves and you know it."

"Shit."

"Yup."

"You're not going to-"

"You bet your sweet ass I am."

"Aww but-"

"No buts. Rix out!"

"What-"

"Nope. Up and out big man."

Even with her arms full of dress Stella managed to pick Quinn up and dump her on a thoroughly confused Rix as he stumbled to stand up and not lose a wriggling and giggling Quinn as they were shoved out the door. He turned just in time to have it slide shut in his face.

"Well." He looked at Quinn's happy little face and she reached to grab at his nose. "I think we just got kicked out."

❧

Two and a half hours later Addy liked what she saw. Her curls had been tamed just enough that the top half were swept up on her head but also trailed down around her face while the bottom half was left free to fall over her shoulders.

The traditional dress of Rix's people made her feel a bit like a Viking bride of ancient times. One shoulder was bare and other only had a strap like a tank top. While it hugged her upper half, at her waist it hung in a free fall that flattered her figure and almost made it look like she had hips. Almost.

Made of long strips of the same leather and soft fabric of Rix's clothes, it also had the same silver metal adorning it like his.

A matching set. A mate set. She grinned at her reflection.

Stella and Addy had decided that a subtle smoky grey around her blue eyes would make them pop but also match the dark of the dress. They'd used a little bit of she didn't want to know what from near one of the electric panels near the door to make it work, Stella saying she'd done something similar once before when she had no makeup on hand. Raking her teeth over her lips would add a little colour, as would pinching her cheeks so they didn't need anything for that.

Who said you couldn't doll yourself up without make-up?

"God you're a bitch for having a complexion like yours. In all the years I've known you I think I've seen you with five pimples. Ever." Affection shone in Stella's eyes as she came up behind Addy to look in the mirror. She cast a critical eye over her handiwork.

"Ok, so. Some ground rules before you two kids head off. No pawing at your hair. I'll not have my work be for nothing. And for the love of god do not make goo-goo eyes at each other and ignore the president. That woman is a bulldog, I swear."

Addy rolled her eyes and chuckled. "Somehow I think my training has prepared me for not getting distracted when 'working'."

"C'mon. Let's go see Rix's jaw hit the floor." Stella grinned and tugged on her hand.

They didn't talk as they made their way to the cafeteria. The eating area seemed to be the main place everyone gathered when they had down time.

"Hang on. Stay here for a sec and come in after me." Stella winked. "Dramatic effect and all." She took off around the corner and entered.

Addy heard Rix's deep voice from down the corridor as she started her grand entrance. "Is Addy far behind you?"

"Nope. She'll be here in a second."

Grinning Addy stepped around the corner and peered through the door but didn't say anything.

ঙ

Rix sat near the door of the cafeteria while the others were spread throughout the room. Quinn played happily with Pravi and Valco at the end of his table.

He turned at the sound of feminine footsteps but was disappointed when he saw it was Stella. She smirked at him, a spark of mischief in her eyes.

He narrowed his eyes. The mouthy female was up to something. "Is Addy far behind you?"

Stella grinned at him.

Yep. The female definitely knew something he didn't.

"Nope. She'll be here in a second." With that, Stella moved to the end of the table with Quinn and the two males she currently had wrapped around her little fingers.

Rix turned, about to say something else when, Valco looked up at something over Rix's shoulder and his jaw dropped.

Whipping his head around, Rix promptly lost the power of thought.

Addy stood just inside the door looking like a male's ideal dream, her pale yellow curls swept up in a way that made him want to thread his fingers through it and tug.

He barely bit back a groan as heat flooded his system.

Gods, the dress. It hung off one shoulder, leaving the other bare except for his mark. She'd hidden it under a wave of curls, but he knew where it was by instinct. The leather and soft fabric hugged her breasts and waist like a second skin before falling to the floor in strips. Rix swallowed harshly.

Females of his kind weren't as curvy as those from Earth. Instead they were nearly as muscled as the males. And fuck if this dress didn't show that completely. He shifted, trying to find some space in his pants as they quickly started to constrict him.

She'd also done something to her face. Her eyes. She'd put something around her eyes. It gave her a powerful but sultry look, something Addy seemed to be reveling in as she took in his reaction.

Ignoring Stella's snicker beside him, Rix growled low as he stood and quickly closed in on his female. More male laughter filled the room, joining Stella's amusement.

Addy raised her hand and kept him at arms length. "Nope. No messing me up! We're already a little late and it took far too long to get this ready." She waved a hand gesturing to herself. "I am *not* starting this over."

She grinned with pure female knowing at his snarl. "Snarl all you like, babe. It's not gonna happen." She leaned around him to peer at Valco and Bran. Both were dressed in similar clothing to Rix, only theirs were missing the metal fastenings. "So you two are joining us I assume?"

Nodding, the males grinned at her. "For dinner with your leader, yes. Copulation, no." Valco laughed deeply at the vicious glare Rix shot at him. "Easy. You may need to change your leathers Captain."

"Watch it Valco."

A small hand rested on Rix's arm, calming him. "They're only teasing." Addy kissed his bicep and grinned. "C'mon. Let's say goodbye to Quinn and get going."

෮෮

They said their goodbyes and Addy checked that Stella would be fine, earning a shove out the door as the red headed tsk'ed at her.

Sitting between Rix and Valco on the transport shuttle, Addy fiddled with her dress nervously. She'd never met the leader of Earth before. Sure, she'd been at the same parties or events but she'd never been introduced face to face. Her father had met and dined with President Gena a year ago after paying for some new medical research facilities.

Rix's big hand enclosed hers and she looked up at him. He smiled down at her, pressing a kiss to the top of her head. "It'll be fine. Stop stressing."

"That's easier said than done." But she smiled at him and rested her head on his   arm and closed her eyes. Maybe if she dozed for the fifteen-minute shuttle ride from Rix's trading shuttle to the presidential cruiser she might be able to calm her nerves.

Doubtful. But hey, she could try. Rix's spicy scent would be a good distraction. She inhaled him. Yep, this was much better than freaking out.

Valco shifted beside her.

Shit. She felt her cheeks flush with embarrassment. "Sorry." She mumbled.

Both males shook their heads as they chuckled. "Do not apologise for loving your male's scent. One should be so lucky to find a female such as you." Valco rumbled, an odd tone in his voice.

Rix squeezed her hands slightly. "I'm sure you'll find a female of strength Valco. Your pretty face should be enough to attract one."

A scowl lit the male's face. "It's because of my face that I attract the females looking for nothing but a pretty hologram to show their Parems."

Extracting a hand from her mate's she touched the big male's shoulder. "I'm sure there will be one worthy of you. We've just got to find her." She winked at him.

Valco smiled at her before his eyes turned thoughtful. "Maybe there's a female that you know that would be suitable?"

Addy paused and thought carefully. "Maybe. But I wouldn't want to get your hopes up. But I'll think on it." She gave his arm a gentle squeeze and smiled at him before laying her head back on her mate's shoulder.

"Docking now." Bran's impossibly deep voice echoed from the pilots' chair.

"Crap. Here we go. Hopefully they don't arrest me for theft."

"They can't. You're *mine* now." Rix all but growled the words in her ear. She shivered at the heat in them.

"Right. But let's wait till we see my parents before we tell the rest of my people that."

The dull knocking noises of the docking bays sealing to one another sounded and Addy stood and faced the rear of their shuttle. A loud hiss sounded as the cabin pressures synchronized, leading to long seconds before the doors lowered into a loading ramp.

A single figure waited for them in the centre of the docking bay.

Chapter 9

Addy sucked in a breath at the sight of her father. His sharp blue eyes took in the three Farskon males behind her. They narrowed at Rix when he noticed her left hand in Rix's.

Well, this was going to be fun.

"Ambassador Rix Nahr I presume." Her father gave a tight nod, then the glint in his eyes softened and he opened his arms. "Addison." He all but breathed her name and she rushed him.

"Dad." She held him as tight as she could. His favourite cologne filled her nose and she sighed deeply.

"Oh chicken." He squeezed her back before holding her face in his hands to study her. "We thought we'd lost you and Quinn. The presidential pod was gone but we couldn't be sure that Alex had gotten you to safety." He crushed her to him again, his cheek resting on the top of her head. They both choked a sob back. "Little Quinnie? Is she with you?" He looked hopefully back inside the shuttle.

Addy wiped at her eyes and hoped she hadn't ruined her improvised makeup. "No, I left her with Stella and the rest of Rix's crew."

"Stella is with you?!" Her father's shocked shout startled her and she jumped before chuckling. Stella was the second daughter Nolan Ward never had.

"Yes. We were watching a holi-vid together when Alex came and rushed us to the presidential suite. He shoved us in the presidential pod and took the staff one himself. I've explained this to about six different generals and officials via coms yesterday. Did they not pass it along to you?" Odd that they wouldn't have shared her report.

Her father frowned. "No. I only knew that you were alive. Not your condition. I didn't even know if you were conscious." He frowned back at Rix and his males. "I bribed the commander meant to receive the Farskon Ambassador, determined to get answers on your condition myself." He grimly studied the males behind her. "I don't care how big they are, I'd have gotten the info I wanted one way or another."

Addy grinned and kissed her father's cheek and gave him another squeeze. "Oh Dad. I'm fine. We're all fine. We stank to high heaven thanks to Quinn's small mountain of used nappies. But we were fine." She glanced back at Rix, who'd stayed at the bottom of the loading ramp giving her space with her father. He showed no emotion and simply waited.

Addy held her hand to him, gesturing for him to join her.

※

Rix couldn't help but admire the steely eyed human male. Just how the small human had expected to get 'info' out of him he wasn't sure, but he understood the sentiment.

He too had frowned when he'd heard that the Earth officials had not passed on Addy's vid reports to her family. Who else had they not shared her story with?

Looking at his males he shook, his head slightly at their silent question. He'd give his mate a moment with her Parem. Instead he took the time to study the male.

Indeed, he had the blue eyes she'd said he would but they were a slightly lighter colour. And harder, not quite as soft as his daughter's. This male was fiercely intelligent. He'd be a tough negotiator. No wonder Addy was so good at the trade deal. Rix also wondered just how wealthy his mate's family was if her father could so easily bribe a commander of the Earth Space Fleet.

Those hard, blue eyes met his over Addy's head and hardened even further. Oh yes. He knew something was between them.

Addy turned back toward him and held her hand out. A quiet

grunt told his males to stay where they were before he stepped off the loading ramp.

His long strides quickly ate up the space between them and he clasped her warm fingers gently.

"Dad." She paused, grinned up at him and took a breath. "Meet your new son-in-law." She winked at him when his eyes widened in surprise. "Rix Narh, this is my father Nolan Ward."

Nolan sucked in a strangled gasp.

He heard Valco chuckle softly behind him.

Addy looked back at her father and Rix could see she was trying not to laugh at her father's expression.

"Think of the trade deals Daddy." Addy chuckled but Nolan coughed and choked. "Breathe Dad. Breathe." She patted his back.

Rix still didn't say anything, unsure of what to do. So he waited for Nolan to recover.

It didn't take long. The older human sputtered for a moment longer before staring at his daughter. Then he pinned Rix with those hard, blue eyes. Rix simply gazed back.

After a few long moments he decided to slowly raise a hand in a gesture he'd seen between human males a couple of times before. "You've raised a strong female."

Nolan cocked his head to the side a little, before he begrudgingly shook Rix's hand a little harder than seemed necessary to Rix.

"You've treated her well?"

"Dad!"

Rix narrowed his eyes at the veiled suggestion that his paring with Addy had been forced and stared off with the human. "Of course. During and after the trade meeting your daughter held my respect. Then when we found her not only alive but with her daughter and friend, Addy truly held my attention." He paused and looked at his mate. His expression softening. "My people know very quickly when we find a potential mate. Once the mating is completed it's irreversible and lifelong, barring death."

Nolan looked shocked. He looked to his daughter. "Are you sure?"

Addy smiled warmly. "Yes Dad. Very sure. You should see how much Rix and the rest adore Quinnie. I'd never leave her alone with them if I wasn't absolutely sure of her safety."

Rix chuckled at the memory of the first time his males had met the little curly haired baby. How was that only three cycles ago?

Nolan stared at him, confused. "What am I missing?"

"Rix and his crew of eight very large scary-looking males all turned to goo the moment they saw Quinn. We stank to high heaven and they all just went to goo. And she wasn't even awake to gummy smile at them. It turns out one of the scariest males had a twin brother that died. His name was Quinn also. The first thing he said when he held her as I got out of the president's pod was 'Any of you make her cry and I'll make you pay.' With an added growl for effect." Addy grinned at her father. "Rix later told me that Ralli is a rather feared assassin on their home world. He's currently babysitting with Stella."

Nolan stared at his daughter and slowly smiled. "I always did tell you to make friends with the meanest looking one in a bad situation."

Addy smiled and nodded, then got a serious look on her face and looked around. "Where's Mum? With Alex I'm guessing?"

"Yes. She's keeping watch over him." A dark look passed over Nolan's face and Rix tensed. Addy saw it too and clenched her fingers in his hand.

"What is it?"

"Come, we'll not talk of this here. Tell your males to follow us if they do not speak the Common. Your dinner has been pushed back half an hour. Follow me to my suite."

"They understand." Rix nodded and the males quickly followed, flanking them as they strode out of the docking back and down the corridor.

"I chose a suite near the D-Bays, knowing you'd ask about your brother." Nolan ushered them into a small crew cabin. It was crowded with the three very large Farskons crammed in. Valco stayed by the door while Bran had to sit on the bed to try and make some room.

"Dad you're scaring me. What is wrong with Alex?"

Rix thought about it a moment. "Someone is trying to pin it on him, aren't they?" Nolan peered up him. "Yes. Due to my son being in a coma he can't defend himself. The military is trying to rush the investigation and are looking at anyone and anything that they can shift the blame onto." Nolan smiled almost cruelly. "What they don't know is that Commander General Kane and I went to grade school together. The moment the shit show of your trade deal went down, he sent a copy of the security footage to me." Addy gasped. "Yes. The trade meeting. The hallway. The secondary meeting after that incident in the corridor. Everything. Highly illegal of him to do so but he didn't like seeing a bruise on my daughter's arm. You may not have actually met him before but he considered you his niece."

Rix smiled. Very smart of the commander general.

Nolan continued. "I spoke with Alex via coms the moment I viewed the footage. He reacted much the same way you are Rix. Do I call you Rix, or Nahr?"

"Rix." Addy answered. "There's more, isn't there Dad."

Nolan held his daughter's shoulder and paused. "It seems my telling Alex of Julius' rule breaking gave him an idea, something that should save both him and you of any coverups from the Star Fleet. After sending you out in the pos, Alex used precious time, and the presidential suite's access to almost all commands, to send the previous two hours' security footage of the bridge as well as opening a live feed to our company servers. I'll have to thank Stella for teaching him how to do it covertly."

Addy's eyes widened and she stumbled. Rix was quick to catch her. "You have footage of the whole Scraver attack."

Nolan's expression hardened. "No. I have footage of my son warning his superiors and being ignored."

"But he said he didn't have time to warn anyone."

"He did. He spotted the markings were off on the vessel hailing the Cruiser and warned the Captain on shift to reconfirm the docking pass." Her father's voice shook with rage. "He ignored Alex as if he hadn't spoken."

"Ah. So that's why he said fuck them."

"Unfortunately, that Captain has friends and relatives in high places that don't want their reputations tarnished with such a huge fuck up."

"And they're trying to clean their hands of it by making Alex the bad guy."

"I think this presidential dinner is a thinly veiled attempt on your life. As the only known survivor to talk to Alex directly, and his sister, I'm certain they're going to assume that you're going to be trouble."

Three low growls filled the small space. Nolan arched a brow and looked to Addy then at Rix.

Bran snorted and spoke first. "Rix is the-"

"Bran!"

Bran shot a glare at Valco and continued. "- is the best warrior after Ralli and me. Even you Valco, a medic are a great warrior - I'm sure we'd be fine. If anyone could protect Ambassador Addison, it would be us. Besides, not many threaten a mate of the Nahr and live." He paused and looked to Rix. "But maybe we should call Craith and Pravi to join us?"

Valco made a face at Bran who ignored him. Addy watched them both closely. Clearly Valco had thought Bran was going to say something else. And "the Nahr" not "a". Was Nahr not Rix's surname but a title? She shot a questioning look at Rix, who shook his head minutely then nodded. Satisfied he'd tell her later, she realised her father had seen her silent conversation. "Maybe later is not the best idea son."

Rix started at Nolan calling him son. Turning to Valco and Bran he frowned.

Addy nearly smiled at Bran who looked almost sheepish. Valco simply glared at Bran.

"For such a quiet male you certainly know when to fuck up by talking too much." Valco shoved at Bran.

Bran growled something low in their native tongue before looking at Rix and lowering his head in what could only be called submission.

"My Father's uncle is the life mate of what you would call our Queen. Though not by blood, I am -" he glanced at Addy, "-was, a favoured heir to the mantle of many high-ranking positions through both mine and the Queen's families. This is not a secret amongst our people. We simply chose not to tell the human officials. Royal connections always cloud the minds of potential traders." He turned and knelt in front of Addy, his height bringing his head in line with her black clad breasts. "After this mess was dealt with I was going to tell you, although personally I think Nahr Nerila will choose my cousin or brother as heir. Not me."

Her blue eyes studied him and she rested her hands on his shoulders. "Nahr is a title, isn't it? Not your name."

"Yes."

"So I guess technically you always had told me of your status. I just didn't understand what Nahr stood for."

The corner of Rix's lips twitched. "True."

"So long as I don't end up queen of another world, I'll forgive you." Addy chuckled and cupped his cheeks in her soft hands. She pressed a light kiss to his lips before withdrawing far too quickly.

Nolan cleared his throat and Rix grunted. They shared a quick glance. Nolan smirked and looked at his daughter. "Well honey, think of the trade deals." He winked.

Valco barked out a laugh before smothering it unsuccessfully with a cough.

Addy chuckled before sobering. "Are you here to give the president the security footage, Dad?"

Nolan embraced his daughter tightly, pressing another kiss to her hair. "I'm here to see you, my daughter, first and foremost. But if you happen to accidentally leave an Orb on the table at the presidential dinner then that's a pure coincidence."

Rix smiled as he stood. "That's sneaky."

Nolan gazed at him a moment before answering. "Maybe. But if it means it'll save my children then I'll do just about anything. Hell, I'll jam that Orb in her face if I have to. I also have a few other Orbs that I'll be 'forgetting' in select places here and there. Or accidentally connect to a cafeteria holi-vid unit."

"I should've brought Stella with me. She could have hacked into a few places for you."

"No no, I'm sure Stella would rather be playing with Quinn." Nolan paused and arched a brow as he eyed Valco. "Although maybe she has other motives for staying with the Farskons if they all look like you three."

Rix snorted. "Stella has her pick of five if she wishes it." He chuckled as Valco growled. "Your human women are dangerously appealing." He smiled as Addy leaned her back against him. She sighed into his embrace.

Chuckling Nolan shook his head. "Just don't meet the other women of privilege from Earth. I've made sure my girl has kept herself grounded and not gotten too preoccupied with the latest fashion trend or gossip scandal. And through her, Stella has stayed grounded too."

An alarm dinged softly, making Nolan turn to a storage unit.

He checked an Orb before handing it to Addy. "I've set this to alarm and then play the footage in about three hours. If you leave this somewhere hidden but in a main area of the president's suite, she should find it."

Addy frowned. "We're having dinner in her personal suite?"

"Gena is a sharp woman. She knows exactly what is up against you. In fact, after asking me to keep you here, she will be the one to accompany you to her suite. She's not taking any chances of someone other than me speaking to you in person first."

Apprehension filled Addy and she looked to Rix. The tension she saw there showed her he had underestimated the risk too. So much for a simple dinner to tell her story. This was sounding more like a private trial.

Before she could gather her thoughts, the door chimed and a heavy weight settled uncomfortably in her gut.

"Don't let her wait, Dad." She took the Orb from her father and stood facing the door. Rix's warm arm came around her waist to rest on her hip, she took strength from   him.

She felt rather than heard the other two Farskon males flank them on either side, Rix's males wordlessly supporting her. Or were they her males now too? Maybe she'd have to ask Rix about that.

Nolan looked back over his shoulder at the little united front his daughter and her mate made. A sly smile spread over his face.

The slight hiss of the door was all that sounded in the small room before sliding back.

ॐ

Nolan nodded respectfully at the slender figure revealed.

"President Gena. May I introduce my daughter Addison Ward and the Farskon Ambassador Rix Nahr." Stepping to the side, he swept a hand in Addy and Rix's direction.

Rix eyed the human female as she paused like she had all the time in the world. He knew it was a subtle reminder that she was in charge on this ship.

President Gena Reynolds wasn't a large woman by any means, only slightly taller than Abby in height. But the air of authority she wielded was almost a tangible being in the tiny room. Her dark hair was wound back in a tight bun at the base of her head, the charcoal of her suit bringing out the chestnut streaks. Grey eyes were steely as she surveyed the room before stepping over the threshold. Staying just inside the tiny crew room she turned to Addy, her dark brow arching when she took in Addy's dress next to Rix's matching leathers. Her lips twitched in what he hoped was amusement.

Yep. This woman was a ball-busting hard ass. And she knew exactly the relationship between Addy and Rix.

"Thank you, Nolan." Pausing, those steel grey eyes rested on the two males behind Addy. "Well, you are large, aren't you?" Her tone was dry, before she settled on Addy. "Ambassadors. Are congratulations in order?"

Addy carefully kept her face blank but Rix chuckled. His fingers tightened on her hip before he let her go to stretch his hand across to the human leader.

"You remind me of my aunt, President Gena." He grinned, flashing fang. "Yes. I've claimed your ambassador."

Addy choked and elbowed him in the ribs. "Rix!"

Gena chuckled, not at all offended with Rix's candidness, and shook his hand, her grip firm despite her small hands. "She's going to need a big male like you in her corner."

And just like that the friendly atmosphere evaporated. Rix kept his smile in place though it no longer reached his eyes. "She has eight." Two low grunts behind him confirmed his statement.

"Good." Grey eyes flicking between the males, the human female drew in a sharp breath. "Before we continue, something needs to be said. I need to thank you and your males for returning to the Earth Cruiser so quickly. Without your people, I doubt we'd have found the few that survived in the ventilation shafts. I may need to have a secondary trade meeting with you about the technology your males used to find them."

Behind him Valco snorted.

Rix growled low in warning. The male better not slip again. He'd seemed to have gotten too relaxed in the last few days.

Gena looked at him questioningly. She seemed to take the growling in stride.

Rix glanced at Addy who simply looked amused, if slightly confused. He cleared his throat.

"We didn't use technology to find those survivors." He tapped his nose. "One of the females had lost the contents of her bladder in her fear at the sounds of our approach. Our heavy feet sound similar to Scraver boots. We scented her."

"Scent?" Gena appeared shocked. "I didn't know your senses were so acute."

"We don't like to broadcast the knowledge. Humans are emotional creatures. Your scents change constantly. It makes it easier during trades to tell what you might be thinking. Or hiding."

"I'm impressed." She turned slightly and looked over her shoulder at the human males she'd had accompany her. "That info is not to be put in any reports by any of you."

Surprised, Rix nodded at the human leader. "Thank you. I appreciate the gesture."

Gena smiled slightly back up at him. "Come. I will ask you to not talk during our journey to my suite. You don't know who is listening on this ship, even if it's mine."

And with that, the small female spun and stepped back out of the room.

The trip through the corridors to President Gena's personal suite was short. Though no one wanted to admit it, all of them were on edge. After her father's warnings of possible assassination plots and cover ups, Addy and the Farskons were on high alert. As instructed by President Gena, no one spoke. Instead they simply followed behind her charcoal suit, the presidential guard surrounding them all. Two in front, three behind with another right beside the President herself.

Addy's belly flip-flopped at every corner, the president's display of tight security emphasising the seriousness of her situation.

Approaching a large set of doors, the guards in front stopped and took positions on either side. Pressing her hand to a touch panel to the right, the president ushered them into her personal suite. "Please, let us eat and talk further in private. My security does sweeps for listening devices hourly." She stopped Rix with a hand on his arm. "I'm going to have to ask that your males wait out here."

Addy turned and watched Rix frown down at her peoples' leader. Coming back to him, she rested her hand on his arm while directing her comment to Gena. "What if we each have one guard inside? On either side of the door?"

Rix shook his head. "I apologise President Gena, but I will not have my males out of my sight. You may bring the remaining four of your men inside if that would make you more comfortable? Mine will stay here by the door." He gestured to the left where a small sofa was placed. Addy assumed its purpose was for those that carried many shopping bags or wished to put on their shoes as before they left the suite, something a president would not be doing.

Gena smiled and took her hand back. "I didn't think you'd go for it, but my security insisted I try anyway." She nodded and moved to the centre of the room where a small dining table had been set up. "Shall we get started while we wait for the food to be served?"

Addy looked about with interest as she took her place. The plush luxury of the room wasn't immediately obvious but it was there in the details, the coverings of the chairs and sofas; the understated lighting and then the sheer expanse of the room itself. When in space, quarters on ships tended to be smaller than one would think, but this could almost be a room in a sprawling mansion.

"Do you like it? This is a prototype for my family's new line of Space Cruisers. There is one of these suites on each level." That explained why they hadn't used a lift on the way here. "While this is a Cruiser, we intend for it to be a fully weaponised battle station as well, with the option of removing the 'Presidential suites' to make more room for crew cabins. We were intending to install your defensive systems, Rix, and then in the future maybe upgrade the weaponry to include some of yours as well."

"How many of these suites are on this particular ship?" Addy was curious. "Thirteen. If reduced to just one there would be room for another forty crew cabins
and two extra cafeterias. But you aren't here for a sales speech for my family's cruise liners." Steepling her fingers against her chin, elbows resting on the tabletop, Gena's grey eyes hardened, her easy manor gone. "You're here because I need answers on what actually happened, and you want to tell your side of the story. Thankfully they should be one and the same."

Taking a deep breath, Addy played with the edge of her father's Orb while at the same time reaching for the warmth of Rix's hand. He gave her a gentle squeeze of reassurance.

Maybe she could just outright show the president the Orb and so the security footage? Do them at the same time. None of the fake 'Oh I left my Orb behind, silly me' business. Steeling herself Addy decided that would be exactly what she'd do. She lay the Orb flat and pushed it slowly across the table.

"Unbeknownst to me my father was childhood friends with Commander General Julius Kane. After the trade deal, one of the generals wasn't happy with me and made it known in the corridor while I was alone. The commander general illegally copied and sent security footage of what took place to my father. Father told Alex of this. When my brother realised what was about to happen, he took that idea of copying footage and ran with it. Using his high security clearance and your presidential suite's access he sent what was happening on the Earth Cruiser to our family servers in real time, including the moments just before this when he warned the captain on deck of what he thought was a threat and was dismissed and then ignored." She tapped the Orb. "It's all on there."

President Gena's eyes locked on the Orb. "Well shit. No wonder your father insisted on being here personally. I was not informed of your being accosted at the trade meeting." Looking over her shoulder Gena addressed one of her men. "Send a squad of your choice to help guard Mr Ward's family. Especially the young commander. He is not to be touched by anyone his father does not permit - and background check everyone who's already come into contact with him." Turning back to the table she played a hand on the blank surface of the Orb but didn't activate it. "Is there anything on here that you can tell me that I won't see?"

The doors to the suite opened as two waiters pushing trolleys entered. The food was first inspected by a presidential guard before being sniffed by Bran. Both nodded and let the waiters pass.

Addy took the moment to think as their entrees were served. "Not that I can think of. Estelle Morgan, the second daughter of Brandon and Vivian Morgan, was in my suite with me. She and my daughter were in your pod with me. We all survived thanks to Alex's quick thinking. Oh, and your pods life support calculations were scarily wrong. Stella corrected them when she hacked into it to activate the distress beacon early. Your husband and father may want those to be checked out properly."

Gena stared at her for a moment, her food forgotten. "Fuck. Estelle Morgan too?" She sat back, crossed her arms and narrowed her eyes at Addy. "The three of you fit in that pod?"

"Even with the dodgy calculations, we had another two days left before anything drastic would have happened. And my daughter Quinn is only eight months old. The pile of used nappies took up more space than she did."

"Jesus. That still would've been tight, for what? Five days?"

Addy nodded. "I also need to thank you - or apologise - for us taking that pod. Alex thought it would be the safest way to save Quinn and I. All the other higher ranked people were in the cafeterias, he said-"

The president grunted, frowning harshly, and threw up a hand to stop Addy. Gena pushed her half-eaten meal away. "Never. Ever. Apologise for that. I can see the sincerity in the way you speak to know that you're telling me the truth. So don't you ever apologise for listening to your quick-thinking brother and saving the life of your daughter and friend. I'm only regretting that my husband listened to my father and didn't put a cloaking mechanism on the staffing shuttle - though that helped us find your brother in the end." Gena's gaze shifted to Rix as Addy gaped at her. "I suppose Miss Morgan is still aboard your shuttle?"

"Yes, she is currently employed by my mate as … Nanny? For Quinn." Addy saw the president was surprised to hear this but was still unable to form a coherent sentence after the lecture she'd just gotten.

"One of the brightest computer programmers of the Morgan company is currently working as a Nanny?"

Addy couldn't help but chuckle, breaking out of her stupor. "Yes. She got a little of sick of data reports and her mother, so she used my husband's death and then Quinn as an excuse to escape earth and her mother's reach."

Gena's hard shell cracked a little when she shuddered. "Oh, that woman is a piece of work." Gesturing at the waiters for their dessert to be served, Gena leaned her elbows onto the table. "Well I'm glad she managed to escape and that the three of you survived. I'll be viewing the footage as soon as you leave. Now please Rix, tell me of your home planet and other niceties. I'd like to think of something fondly later when I get angry watching this." She tapped the Orb and leaned back as the waiters served fancy looking chocolate ice cream, complete with a little mint leaf on the top and dark, silky chocolate sauce dripping down the sides.

Chapter 10

Rix was trembling. He wasn't entirely sure why but a few minutes ago on the shuttle ride back to his ship he'd noticed his body wasn't quite right. There seemed to be something fuzzy around the edges of his vision.

Something was off.

They had finished off their dinner with the human president with small talk, swapping stories of their worlds. Both Addy and Gena were bursting with curiosity and lapped up his every word. Then after making arrangements to have another face-to-face meeting in a few days, they were escorted back to their shuttle. Nolan had been waiting, saying that he'd kept an eye on the shuttle to make sure no one tampered with it. He also admitted he wanted to say goodbye to Addy again.

Rix started bouncing his leg on the ball of his foot. He felt like he'd just woken up from a perfect nap after eating some Sangri fruit. He was energised beyond belief. Tapping his fingers on his bouncing leg, he barely bit back a growl at Bran. Fuck, how slow was he going?

"Rix? Are you ok?"

Addy's sweet voice broke through his energised haze, his vision suddenly snapping crystal clear as he slowly looked down at her beside him.

A wave of heat hit him like a freight liner. Dear Gods.

His eyes locked onto the swell of her breasts, the black leather of the Larki from his home planet hugging her like it was suctioned on.

Suction. Gods what he wouldn't give right now to have his mouth suctioned onto her pretty little pink tips. A low growl rumbled from deep in this throat.

"Uh Rix. Look at me." Concern filled her voice.

"Hmm, I am."

A chuckle came from the front of the shuttle. "Keep it in your pants, Nahr. We're docking now."

Bran's deep voice was like a shock of cold water. What the hell was going on with him? He was ready to strip his mate bare and rut at her right there in the middle of the shuttle floor, his males be damned.

"Valco. I need to know what was in the final meal." Valco's head whipped around to look at him.

"What?"

"The food, what was in it?"

"Chocolate ice cream, dark chocolate sauce and a mint leaf garnish." Addy answered before the male could but she was clearly confused. "Chocolate is rare on my planet now. It used to be around in abundant amounts but it only grows in a tiny region of my planet now. It was incredible that the president would share some with us. I don't even want to know how much it cost."

"Chocolate I've had before at the dinner with Narh Nerila. It had been a gift from your leader when our races first met." Rix shuddered as another wave hit him. "Addy, I need you to sit over on the other side of Valco." He gripped the edge of his seat so tight his knuckled cracked.

Everything in his system screamed in alarm as his mate slowly got up and moved to the seat furtherest from him. Her scent was clogging his nose and he was sure there wasn't a spare atom of space in his pants, his cock so hard he was seeing spots around the edges of his too-sharp vision.

"Gods, Rix, what is wrong with you?" Valco's voice held concern.

"The green leaf on the dessert. What was it?" Hanging his head between his knees, he ground the words out. He still bounced his leg, faster now. His voice was a barely understandable rumble.

"Mint. It was mint. What the fuck is going on?!" Addy touched his arm. Shit. Just that small touch sent wave after wave of sensation through him. Why wasn't she still   on the other side of Valco?

"Judging by the scent he's givin off, he's aroused. Incredibly so."

Shudders racked Rix's frame. Everything trembled. But he was acutely aware of his mate. Even with his eyes clamped shut he knew exactly where she was. Gods he could hear her heartbeat. The sound of her hair as it shifted when she moved slightly.

"The moment we dock properly get her away from me."

"WHAT?!"

Addy's shout nearly made him jump out of his seat. He cringed as his ears twanged painfully. Apparently they were sensitive now too. Her touch left his arm but it still tingled. What in the hell was this?

༚

Rix looked like he was going to rip his seat off the side of the shuttle, his hands were clamped around it so hard. The pain of his face and the way he hunched over made her gut tighten. What was wrong with him? Why didn't he want her to help him?

Addy looked at Valco, but the worry on his face didn't make her feel any better. The big male crouched in front of Rix and the two murmured softly to one another for long moments.

Staying where she was in the seat as far from Rix as the little shuttle would allow, she kept watch out of the corner of her eye and instead watched Bran docking the shuttle. He opened the shuttle door. The moment he hit the door command the big male was out of his seat and came straight to her.

"I'm sorry Addy but I'm going to have to pick you up." Bran's black eyes softened. "He's likely to come at you so aggressively he could hurt you. And that would make him upset."

"What? What do you mean?"

Valco stood, squarely placing his body between Bran and Rix. He ignored the growl that came from behind him. "Something in that food seems to have effected his hormones. He's both super aroused and aggressive."

Addy didn't know what to say. "Oh."

Valco smirked. "You could almost say he's in something similar to a breeding heat. Even though we don't have that."

Uh. What? Holy shit. Did that mean what she thought it did? And from *mint*?

She didn't get to think much as a vicious snarl ripped from Rix. He moved fast and before she could gasp, Valco and Bran were on their asses, practically thrown across the room. Large hands clamped down on the top of her arms, though she couldn't help but think how gentle Rix was when he pinned her against the wall. Aggressive yes. But in a hard way, gentle too. She cupped his forearms, trying to ground herself as best she could.

His golden eyes were practically neon. A strange orange glow emitting from them. His lips were drawn back in a sneer, but he wasn't snarling.

Gods. He was purring. And practically vibrating with it. Waves rolling through his hard body as it pressed against hers from chest to foot.

Soon her breathing was as ragged as his. She licked her lips and that strange orange gaze watched every slow movement of her tongue.

So she did it again.

She didn't think it was possible but Rix ground into her harder. His purring devolved into a low rumble.

"Holy fuck." Someone whispered. It was late and she hoped Stella and the others hadn't come to the loading dock to greet them.

"Out."

"What?"

Addy cleared her throat, never taking her eyes off Rix, who hadn't moved. He seemed content to have her pinned where she was as he started to nuzzle her neck. "Both of you. Get. Out."

"But-"

She cut Valco off. "He won't hurt me. He's *not* hurting me. Go." She toed off her shoes and thanked Rix's people for having a traditional dress with a thigh high split. Slowly she bought her legs up around his hips.

All three males let out a strangled moan. Though Rix's quickly changed into a snarl. "Out." The word was barely understandable, his growl was so deep.

"Shit. C'mon Valco. If either of us see any more of her leg Rix will kill us and you know it." Bran grabbed Valco and hauled him to his feet while dragging him out of the shuttle. "We'll stay close. If he starts hurting you-"

"I'll shout code red." Ha, she had a safe word. Addy snickered and ground herself against the hard bulge nestled against her sex. "Now get out. And don't listen too hard."

A soft hiss sounded as the door closed. And instantly two things happened. Rix all but dropped her on her ass back down on the seat. And he dropped to his knees on the floor in front of her.

That strange orange glow locked on the apex of her thighs, her dress having been pushed up around her hips. The black lace of her panties were clearly visible. Why she had been watching holi-vids with Stella wearing black lace that night she had no idea, but with how Rix was now looking at the only set of sexy underwear she had, Addy was anything but sorry. He looked like he was desperate to develop x-ray vision.

"Hmm, do these need to come off?" Addy hooked a thumb and tugged slightly at the lace. Rix's purrs grew and filled the room. Slowly, almost as if he was worried he'd scare her, he lifted a hand. "Uh-uh. No." With her other hand she pushed his raised hand away from her. He growled. "I'll do it. If you like these, let's not rip them." She winked at him.

Lifting her butt off the seat she slowly wriggled, shifting her panties down past her knees to catch on her ankles. Her wriggling also brought her to the edge of the shuttle seat and she slumped back, awkwardly leaning right back against the wall she'd been pinned against. The purrs started to thrum. But still Rix did not touch her, but simply stared at her like a man starved. She felt her arousal spike. Brazenly she let her thighs fall wide, exposing herself to that orange glow.

"Mine." Rix growled and clamped his mouth over her making her breath hitch. He sucked hard on her.

"*Yes!* Yours." She moaned and threaded her fingers through his soft hair. His tongue was relentless as he lapped at her. She couldn't think with the vibrations from his purrs sliding down his tongue straight to her swollen clit. The pleasure was so intense she moaned again.

Rix's hands slid up her legs to the inside of her thighs. She threw her head back in a silent scream when a thick finger entered her, hitting that spot deep inside. Then another finger joined the first. Over and over he lapped at her while his fingers hit her G-spot. Purring and growls faded to the background, she didn't even hear her own almost constant moaning. Climax hit when Rix gently bit her clit. Addy screamed and would've slammed her legs shut around Rix's head if he didn't have had her pinned open to him. Still he licked at her, drawing wave after wave out of her orgasm.

"Holy shit." She whispered and slid down the wall to awkwardly lay along the seats. Rix was still purring. Jesus, his fingers were still inside her. She jerked when he slowly lapped from where his fingers disappeared in her to her clit. She was oversensitive. Not painfully so but wow. She swore she could almost feel each of his taste buds.

Another lap of his tongue had her groaning. She made a fist a hand in his hair and held him still. Or tried to. He snarled and did it again.

"No. Please. I'm sensitive."

Rix simply moved his fingers inside her instead. He licked the soft skin of her inner thighs, his fangs dragging along her. Goosebumps sprang up on her legs and she shivered. Her hands were still locked in his hair so she tried to drag his head up to her.

He relented but moved at his own pace, nuzzling her stomach and tonguing her navel, those two fingers still fucking her lazily as he nibbled his way up her body.

δ♥

Dear gods.

He wanted to feast on Addy for the rest of his life. The urge was so intense it was almost as if someone else was controlling him.

But it seemed that as long as his nose or mouth was filled with her, he could sort of think. Almost. Maybe.

Alright, no. But at least he could kind of control himself. A little. At least he had his purring under control.

"Something I ate has sent me crazy." He mumbled it against the underside of her breast. The skin there was so soft. He licked it, loving the taste of her.

"Really? I'd never have guessed." Addy's quiet chuckle made her breast jiggle against his lips. Mmmm. "You nearly fucked me with an audience."

"Mmmm. I haven't actually taken you yet." He slid his fingers in and out of her wet heat. In and out, in and out. "But at least I can speak in sentences now." He licked her again.

He raised his head to look at how she was sprawled on the shuttle seats. Removing his fingers from her, he sucked them clean and moaned at the taste of her. Another wave of heat crashed through him. With his spare hand he lifted her left leg and layed it along the seats against the wall. He left her right one hanging off the side, leaving her spread for him. He shoved his pants down around his thighs and ripped his shirt over his head before maneuvering himself over her.

The head of his cock landed right where it needed to be and he snarled as her arousal slicked over him. Fuck.

The waves of heat nailed him in the back with double the intensity of before. He shook with the force of holding himself back and it took everything he had not to slam inside Addy's tight little pussy as fast and hard as he could.

"I hope I can think properly after this." Lowering himself he slid the head of his cock inside her. He dropped his head and kissed the flesh of her exposed shoulder. Addy arched under him, the movement making him sink deeper inside her.

"Please Rix. Move in me."

Those three soft words snapped his control. He thrust himself inside her slick channel and they both gasped when he bottomed out. Pulling almost all the way out, he almost relished the freedom of moving as hard as he could as he thrust back inside her heat, over and over. His purring mixed with her near-constant moans until neither could understand who made what noise.

Addy's blunt teeth bit down on his arm as she came, her scream muffled by his flesh. Her inner muscles clamped around his cock and he roared as spots clouded his vision and his climax sizzled through him, frying what seemed like every nerve he had.

It took long moments before Rix was aware of Addy stroking his back. From his shoulder to his butt, her soft touch trailed over him. Immediately he pushed himself up and off her upper body. Shit he'd just taken her as hard as he could without a thought for her.

She moaned quietly as he stumbled back off her before landing on his ass in the middle of the shuttle floor. His pants were still caught around his thighs.

Fuck how badly had he hurt her? She still hadn't opened her eyes.

Of course, that was the moment she did open them. She grinned at him sprawled on the floor beside her and then stretched her arms above her head, her back arching and her little toes pointing. She groaned again.

"Mmmmm. You should do that more often." He sat there starring at her.

"What?"

She chuckled at him. "I said you should do that more often. Lose control. Holy fuck." She stretched out again. "But maybe in the comfort of an actual bed."

He couldn't quite process what she was saying. His mind was still fried from the explosive climax. At least he couldn't feel any of the intense waves of heat. Yet. He had a feeling they'd be back.

"You- you're not hurt? I didn't hurt you?"

"Mm no. Destroyed me maybe. But didn't hurt me."

"Destroyed?"

"Yup. Forever."

Huh?

"You've just raised the bar so high I don't think you're ever going to live up to that level of 'Oh my god' ever again." Humor filled her voice as she smirked slyly at him.

"What?"

Addy's musical laughter filled the room. "Oh babe. You're truly sex fried, aren't you?"

He mustn't have hurt her too badly if she was laughing at him. To be sure, he sat up properly and pulled his pants up over his ass. He grimaced as the soft material touched his cock. Gods, he was sensitive. Walking was not going to be easy. He knelt by Addy as she tried to pull her dress into place while still laying down.

"Can you find my panties for me?" Rix couldn't help but grin when he spotted them caught halfway up the shuttle wall above her.

He pointed and they both chuckled. "Oh."

Snagging her panties, he helped her fix her dress which was also a good way to check Addy over. She'd have a few bruises but otherwise seemed unharmed.

Unable to resist he leaned over and tasted her lips again and barely held back a groan when she licked and nipped at his lower lip. Damn, they were going to have to get moving and get somewhere with a bed. Now.

Scooping her up into his arms, he smiled when Addy chuckled and wound her arms around his neck, her head resting against him. Rix turned and triggered the door. He completely ignored his men, who were gathered around waiting for them.

"Move. I can think but this hasn't passed." He kept going and made his way toward his rooms, shouting over his shoulder as he went. "Please watch Quinnie for a while longer."

Addy shifted in his arms and her lips found his neck.

"I'll be fine." She called out.

6❧

Rix lay on his back in an unused crew cabin about one corridor from the docking bay. The bed didn't even have any coverings - if you didn't count his and Addy's shredded clothes. It had taken another three rounds of sex for the effects of the mint to wear off. While he hadn't been as aggressive, his need for her was still extremely intense.

A herb? Addy had said the mint was a herb. He'd nearly lost his mind due to a garnishing herb. And that it was used in many human dishes, mostly sweet desserts. And that it was not as rare as the chocolate.

Jesus, they were going to have to send out a message for all future meetings to *not* have any mint in their catering. He imagined the mess that could cause if even one of his males ate it accidentally. Rix has eaten only one small leaf, but Addy said it was often used in much larger quantities.

"Are you also realising how much of a mess this mint thing could cause?"

Rix looked over at a sleepy-looking Addy stretched out beside him in the dim cabin. "We need to send a message to your father straight away. He's medically qualified. We could pretend I had a mild allergic reaction due to the single leaf."

Addy rolled onto her side. "I was thinking the same thing." She stroked a hand down his arm before pressing a kiss to his chest. "C'mon. We'd better go show everyone that you haven't sexed me into a coma. What time is it anyway?"

Addy looked down at the tattered remains on the bed and mourned the loss of the traditional dress. She hoped Stella would be able to make another from the stored female outfits the ship had.

"There should be some basic clothes in the storage compartments of this cabin. I'll find them." Rix rose to his full height and stretched. "Damn, that stuff is potent."

Addy chuckled. "It appears we've found a natural Farskon viagra." She laughed harder at Rix's confused expression. "It's a drug human males take to improve their sexual performance."

Rix grunted. "I, for one, never want to experience that again. It was painful. And

worse, I feared I would hurt you, but I didn't care. I just needed release." He rummaged around as he spoke pulling out pieces of clothing. He held a couple out to her.

"Here. You are right. We'd better go and sort this mess out."

⚬⚬

It took hours. Explaining everything. Taking blood samples.

Sending messages to both Addy's father and President Gena. Finally getting cuddles with Quinnie after what seemed like days but was only a night and some of the morning. Then it was more reports and questions and getting results back.

Apparently mint seemed to be something of a sexy catnip to Farskons. Odd but hey, aliens react in weird ways to foreign substances, right? Either way, Addy wasn't complaining too much, now that she knew what it was. However, she and Stella had decided to throw away the unopened mint flavoured toothpastes sent by their families. Addy wasn't entirely sure Stella had actually done it though.

Then it was more cuddles and some quiet catch-ups, but finally Addy was snuggled in Rix's bed with her baby girl softly snoring away beside her.

While Addy and Rix had been stuck sorting out what everyone now called the Mint Mess, Stella and the rest of the crew moved Addy and Quinn's things into the shuttle's captain's suite. When Quinnie was old enough she could now have her own room off Rix's ... hers ... their sitting room. There were also unused suites adjacent that they could alter and make a part of theirs if they needed to in the future.

Addy smiled at the thought of possibly having babies with Rix. Maybe she should've kept her toothpaste for making that happen?

Addy rolled over and wished Rix wasn't still stuck doing yet more reports on the effects of the mint for his own people's medical records. Both he and Valco felt it should be done now while the details and sensations were still fresh in case anyone came into contact accidentally. Mint flavouring really was just about everywhere.

She sighed and shifted again, but was fast asleep by the time Rix finally joined her a few hours later.

Rix looked down at his little human family and smiled. Addy

would be overjoyed when she discovered his little surprise tomorrow.

"Valco, would you accompany us? Maybe your medical training has something ours does not." Addy looked hopefully at the large male across the cafeteria. Rix nodded thoughtfully beside her as he handed Quinn another slice of fruit.

"This would be smart. Even if you just looked around their medical suites, it could still be educational for you."

Valco grinned sheepishly at them. "I was actually hoping you'd ask. I would love to." Addy nodded, pleased. With the addition of Valco, that meant there'd be her and Rix, Quinn and Stella, Ralli, and then finally Craith going to visit her brother. Gorven, Pravi, Bran and Harthi were going to stay on the ship, with an open comm to Rix's brother Nixa. No one knew what was going to happen but after the Mint Mess and a few other reports over the last two days from Rix, Nixa had taken their family cruiser and travelled to just outside of the reach of Earth's radar, hiding at the edge of the Milky Way in a small collection of asteroids. He would be close if needed.

Addy wasn't sure what that meant but she felt better knowing that more of Rix's people - family, at that - were close.

"Did anyone speak to Stella before we got here for breakfast?" Addy wanted to help her friend pack the baby bag before they left, and it was odd that she wasn't here already.

Craith coughed quietly from a table near buffet. "We received a vid late last night from Stella's family. Your father must've let them know she was alive. They must be relieved. I gave it to her this morning, but I haven't seen her since."

"Shit." Addy quickly scooped up another mouthful of food before kissing Rix and then Quinn. "Will you be ok with Quinn for a bit? I'm willing to bet that vid wasn't from her family, but from her mother. I wonder what the hell that bitch had to say this time. Stella has had good reason to not tell her family she survived just yet.

"Christ, I bet that monster of a woman was angry because she now has to stop using the sympathy of Stella being attacked or dead to further her company's appeal to the consumer market seeing as she's actually alive and well. Or some such shit."

Addy paused when she heard a clatter of utensils. Craith looked appalled. "Did I do something wrong by giving it to her?"

"No! No, no, in fact I'm glad you waited until this morning. At least she got the night to sleep, without her mother's scratchy voice in her head."

"You do not make this woman seem appealing." Valco looked confused. "Is she not Stella's biological mother?"

Addy grimaced. "Oh, she is. She just has no capacity for emotion for anyone other than herself. I'll explain it later. Wait." She rushed back to Quinn and Rix. "On second thought, I think Stella might need some Quinnie cuddles."

Rix smiled and held his little stepdaughter up. "Quinnie cuddles make everything better. Go. Help Stella. We'll get ready."

As she hurried down the corridor Addy could only imagine the horrible messages Stella must've gotten from her mother. While her father was a cold man, nothing could compare to the sheer calculating meanness of Vivian Morgan.

She reached Stella's door and hit the chime, before opening the door and entering anyway.

She couldn't see Stella in the main living space but could hear the shower unit running. Crap. Not a good sign. But before she could take more than a step or two, the water stopped.

"Stella?" She tapped on the bathroom door. "You ok in there?"

It took a moment before there was an answer. "Yeah." Came the muffled reply. "Two secs."

The door slid open and Stella stood there in a towel, bent over as she wrapped another around her head, twisting and flipping it over as she stood up straight again. "What's up?"

"What? What's up?" Addy put her hands on her hips. "Craith just told me you got a vid from your family. Which I'm guessing was really the bitch queen. I'm here to see if you're ok?" She huffed.

Stella just grinned at her. Then her friend launched herself at her. "Oh, Addy I'm great!" Addy stood frozen in Stella's damp embrace completely confused. "I'm fucking wonderful!"

Stella grabbed her by the hands and spun her in a circle before dancing around the living space.

"Because I've been dead for nearly a week my mother was forced to dissolve my arranged marriage bullshit thing!" Stella's thrilled laughter filled the room. "Isn't that just the best thing in the bloody universe?!"

"WHAT?" Stella was engaged in an arranged marriage?! "You were getting married?"

Stella paused in her dancing and came back to Addy. Taking her hand, she led them both to the couch. Addy sat and watched her friend try to find the right words.

"A couple of years ago Mother was introduced to one of her 'friend's' sons. She seduced him naturally, but at the same time she decided he'd be the perfect match for my red hair. And by having me marry him, her little toy boy would be on hand to scratch that itch if need be." Stella looked disgusted. "It gets worse. He told me this himself when she let him into my apartment at 6.30am to introduce him to me. She just opened the door, waved her 'toodloo' wave and walked back out again. And he, that slime, stared at her ass the whole time. Then looked at me with the same "I'm perfect" smirk." She got up and started pacing, her good mood evidently gone as Addy watched the anger put a flush of colour on her friends' features. "And then! And then he goes 'So apparently I'm your fiancé.' As if I'd just jump into his arms and consummate our new relationship right then and there on my antique Persian rug!"

Stella was breathing heavily glaring at the wall while Addy tried to find her voice. "Then about a week later you provided me with your engagement news. So, I immediately flew to you to celebrate and escape. You were so happy with Graham, I couldn't ruin your newly engaged glow with my mother's drama. I refused to let her be a part of your celebrations. So, I didn't tell you." Still processing, Addy stayed quiet as Stella came to sit with her. "And then it was just the wrong time. And then Graham died. And then you found out you were pregnant. And I just…" She looked lost for a moment. "I didn't want to bring my drama with me, so I just didn't."

"Stella...holy shit." Addy still didn't know what to say. What could she say to all that? Stella had certainly cut through the shit she was sure was piled all through that story.

Stella smiled sheepishly "I might've played into my mother's ridiculous opinion of you, and made you look even more, um, how did she always put it? Incompetently spoilt?" She shook her head. "And pretended that you wouldn't be able to cope without me. And I ran away from it all. My mother; the sleazy idiot she picked out for me; her incessant wedding planner. I ran away from it all and fell in love with a beautiful little girl that I've tried to shower with as much love as possible."

Stella reached out and held onto Addy hands. "Please don't hate me for using you as an excuse to run away."

Addy simply yanked her childhood friend in for a hard-squeezing hug. "Stella. I could never hate you. But why didn't you just tell me all of this? Did you ever consider that I'd have loved to use your drama to escape my drama?" She chuckled darkly and blinked back tears. "I've known you since we were six, which means I know your mother. If I'd known this shit was happening, I could've pretended I needed you as my tech expert for my ambassador support team or some such shit. I'd have gotten you away from the sleazy toy boy the week you met him!"

Laughing, Stella hugged Addy again. "Oh, I wish I'd thought of that! Instead I stewed on it for far too long. Wait!" Stella glanced around. "What time is it?! Shit! I need to get dressed, don't I?" Jumping up, she clutched at the towel around her. "Quick! Help me get my clothes!"

Chapter 11

"You could stay out here with us indefinitely." Rix's suggestion was met with silence. During the first half of the transport shuttle's trip from the Farskon ship, Stella told Rix and the others about her mother's arranged marriage set-up and, along with Addy, tried to explain what her mother was like. But after many many growls and outraged comments, she gave up and instead tried to change the subject to how she now didn't have to worry about that.

"What?" Stella looked up from fidgeting with her dress. Both she and Addy wore a slightly less formal version of the traditional dress Addy had worn to her meeting with the President. Quinn wore a miniature one with little black leggings like Addy's to match Rix's status. Stella's was a muted, soft grey which matched the outfits Craith and the other males wore. Addy cuddled Quinn closer as her little toddler started to fall asleep.

"Well, while Addy and I would be doing the negotiating we're going to need experts from both planets to help translate the defence systems from our tech language to yours. Pravi could start teaching you the differences in programming now if you wish?"

Addy smiled as Stella's face lit up. "You mean it?!"

Addy quickly patted a startled Quinn back to sleep but grinned at Stella's reaction. Rix nodded, happy that Stella liked his idea. "Well, that and we still need a Nanny for Quinn too - although I think the rest of my males could take over that job occasionally when you're busy helping with the installations."

"Dammit, why'd you tell me this now?" Stella wriggled excitedly in her chair. "Now I wanna go back to the ship and start learning your language. Don't get me wrong - I love Quinnie - but I have been itching to have a look at the insides of your ship since I got   out of that pod. I'm just curious to compare our programming styles even though they're from two different worlds." She grinned widely.

"Now you've got her started, she's never going to let it go." Addy chuckled.

"If you want to look so badly, go up to Ralli. He can give you access to the shuttle's internals and keep you busy for the next few minutes until we reach your president's Cruiser."

Stella squeaked and struggled to get out of her strappings while the males chuckled. She quickly joined Ralli and took the copilots seat. "Ooh I could sit here for days. But I'll only take a quick look, I want to see Alex too before I fall down this rabbit hole."

Craith looked to Addy confused. "Rabbit hole?"

"There is an old children's story on Earth, a girl called Alice falls down a Rabbit burrow - that's a small digging mammal's nesting hole - and she goes on a crazy and wonderful adventure. Stella's idea of a wonderful adventure is learning a completely new language while also learning a foreign way to computer program at the same time." Addy smiled with amusement as Craith and Valco's eyes widened. "Yeah, she's a bit crazy. But smart too." She patted Quinn gently and made a mental reminder to find a copy of the story to read to Quinn again. She'd left her last one on the earth cruiser.

Craith was the first to find his voice. "She's quite the female. We didn't realise she was a programming expert." He looked over to where Stella sat with her nose all but pressed into the screen of the shuttles' piloting console. "She never mentioned to any of us that she wished to work on our ship. Pravi will indeed be happy to work with her."

"Maybe she can have a look at my medical equipment. They've been malfunctioning a little the past few days. I might have my human calculations not quite right." Valco scratched the back of his neck under his braid.

Stella's head popped up. "Of course, Valco! You know I hacked into the escape pods life support and found it wasn't correct. I'd love to check it for you." She winked at the big male.

"Thank you, Stella." Valco blushed and nodded his head in appreciation.

"We'll be coming up on the president's Cruiser in a few minutes Rix." Rallli's deep voice filled the small shuttle. "Docking in about eight minutes."

"Wow. It's almost as big at the Earth Cruiser Addy. Come and see it." Stella watched in wonder as they rounded one of the four stationed battle cruisers surrounding President Gena's family's newest cruiser model.

"Holy crap. I don't need to. I can see it from back here." Addy leaned as far forward as her straps would allow without dislodging her sleeping daughter. She moved the baby a little to lay her across her lap and cradle her little head in the crook of her elbow.

"And I'd rather that you stayed in your seat while carrying Quinn, to avoid the possible turbulence caused by that huge ships' stablisers. We have to travel along the side of the ship for a little distance this time, due to our approach." Rix laid a hand on Addy's knee, and rubbed Quinn's sleeping form with his left. The tattoos snaking down his arms flexed as he gave Addy's knee a gentle squeeze. "Last time we were able to approach directly and leave the same way. Now that the last of the battle stations have arrived there is no direct flight path to the Cruiser. Smart but annoying. And I very much doubt that they would come back here with all of the ships currently clustered around."

"I thought the same thing. They tend to hit a ship and then leave that area alone for a long time before they venture back again." Addy laid her head on Rix's shoulder carefully. While Stella hadn't spent as much time perfecting her curls as for the dinner the other night, she had given strict instructions to not wreck her work. Addy tracked the tattoos over the dark skin. She'd yet to have seen the other males' bare arms to know if they had markings like the ones covering her mate's arms.

A small shudder shook Rix's body and Addy looked up. "Sorry, I didn't mean to tickle you with my hair."

Rix smiled as he looked down to her. "You didn't. I like you leaning on me. The shuttle is shaking."

Addy looked back out the portal. The side of the Cruiser filled the entire thing. Addy gasped and realised if the portal had been like a window on Earth she'd be able to lean out and touch the side of the massive ship.

"Jesus! No wonder you said we'd get turbulence! We're insanely close!"

Ralli chuckled. "I might not be the best pilot in this crew but I'm definitely the second best. No one tell Harthi I said that." He pressed a couple of buttons and murmured into the com unit he wore. "Rix - we've been directed to a different docking bay this time."

"Bay 4F?"

"Yes."

"Continue." He looked back to Addy. "We'll be on the same level as your brother's medical unit. I was sent directions from the president and then your father last night. We'll have an escort but I will know if he tries to lead us in a different direction."

"You spoke with Dad?"

"No, it was a written message."

Addy nodded. That was a good idea from the two of them.

"Establishing com connection with Nixa. He'll be able to hear everything I can from now on." Ralli continued to man the controls. "Docking now."

As she listened to the muffled noises of the shuttle docking Addy slightly squeezed Quinn's little hand. She was nervous to see her brother laying in a medical bed covered in tubes and wires. He was always filled with so much life and energy. It would be weird to see him still and quiet. She looked down at her daughter's sleeping form. Reminded of her brother, even asleep Alex snored like an eighty-year-old man. To see him quiet while in a coma would be strange.

Rix gave her another squeeze and kissed the top of her head. "It'll be fine. I'm sure you will be happy to see him, in any condition."

Addy just nodded mutely.

6❧

The added security seemed to be for nothing as they made it to the medical wing in minutes. The soldiers followed and didn't try to lead them at all. Nor did they talk.

They entered the medical wing through the large clear double doors and Rix immediately turned left. Two more guards stood on either side at the start of a short corridor. "Look for suite 6d. Your father said this entire hall had been emptied for your mother and his personnel so they could be on hand at all times." He nodded to the guards by the door. "Bluebird sent seven eggs your way."

The guards nodded and gestured for them to enter.

Stella looked at Addy wide-eyed. "Gena sent her own men?"

"Yes. I forgot to tell you. With codes and all." Addy paused by one of the men. "Thank you for your time here." The soldier nodded and smiled at her for a moment. He quickly wiped the expression from his face and gestured with his head for her to keep moving as Valco stepped up close behind her.

Rix stood at the end of the corridor bearing a large 6D at her eye height. He held out his hands for a still sleeping Quinn and they transferred the little girl into her new father's big arms. Rix gave her a quick kiss before he looked at Addy and stepped back from the door. He nodded to his males behind her and Stella.

"Ralli will stay out here and Craith and Valco will stay out by the door unless you wish for Valco to check over your brother."

The males murmured their agreements and Addy reached out, but the door opened before she could touch the pad.

"Addy."

Her mother hadn't changed in the six months since Addy had last seen her. Her hair wasn't as blonde as it once had been, but that wasn't entirely new either. The pale white streaks did nothing to diminish her mother's natural beauty. Her warm brown eyes filled, and she yanked Addy in for a crushing hug. Nope. Nothing had changed. She was still a scary strong woman. Addy gasped for breath.

"Mum. Mum! I can't breathe!" But she made no move to get away and she just hugged her mother back. The crashing hold eased a little and she sucked in a deep breath, mostly to try and stem the tears she too had filling her eyes. "I'm okay, Mum. We're all okay."

She was squeezed tight again for a second. "I was terrified that we would never find you." Pulling back, Layla cupped her daughter's face and really looked at Addy. She tilted her head and smiled. "You look happy. Your father told me the reason for that." She grinned and winked. Then she turned that assessing gaze on Rix, but didn't let go of her daughter. Instead she tucked Addy in close, an arm around her waist.

Smiling, Addy watched as Rix smiled stepped closer. "Hello. I believe it is customary for a hug but my arms are a bit full at the moment." He lifted Quinn slightly, as she continued to softly snore and snuggled further into Rix's arms.

"Well, we wouldn't want to wake a little Miss Quinnie." Layla leaned forward and pressed a soft kiss to her granddaughter's forehead. "Come in. There's a soft chair with plenty of pillows that we can use to make a little bed for her." She gave Addy another quick squeeze before turning and walking into the suite.

Addy followed and saw that not only was there a comfy chair

full of pillows but her mother had already fashioned them into a little bed. She studiously ignored the rest of the room and instead she helped Rix nestle Quinn, her back purposely to the bed where she knew her brother would be. Glancing up at Rix, she took a deep breath and turned around.

And promptly screamed.

"You're awake?!" She yelled at her smiling brother. "Shit!" She spun and saw that Rix was already checking on Quinn who hadn't flinched in her sleep. Turning, Addy rushed the bed and jumped on her brother.

"Oof! You're heavy, Adds." Alex grinned and patted his sister on the head.

Stella entered the room after talking with Ralli for a moment. She moved to the other side of the bed to Addy and piled on top of the siblings.

Layla stood from leaning over her granddaughter and bumped her shoulder into Rix's. "I thought we sent the message saying that Alex woke up last night?" She looked up at him. "You didn't tell her." It wasn't a question.

"She was asleep. And I thought it would be a nice surprise."

"Surprise indeed." Layla smiled and watched her children hug and murmur to one another. "I believe I owe you some thanks."

Rix looked down in surprise. He opened his mouth but was cut off.

"Firstly, you defended my daughter on that first day in the hallway. And then you found her floating around in space in that tiny pod." Turning, she regarded Rix. Her resemblance to her daughter was uncanny, though in a steely way. This woman was just as shrewd as her husband, while being as warm as her daughter. Layla reached out and laid a hand on his shoulder. "And lastly, you fully accepted my granddaughter whole heartedly and without a second thought. That is not something many men would do. And it's clear the affection Quinn has for you already. I saw how she snuggled into you when I opened the door. So, I say again. Thank you. My daughter is certainly lucky to have found a male such as you." She smiled warmly at him, gripping his shoulder tightly for a moment.

Rix didn't know what to say. He just stared down into the eyes of his new human mother of law - or that was what he thought she was now.

"I hear I need to speak with you ambassador."

"Alex!" Addy sat on the edge of the bed and slapped at her brother's chest.

"Well, I go to sleep for a week and a bit and suddenly you're married and somehow an ambassador to two worlds?" Alex looked between Addy and Rix.

Rix smiled. Nolan and Layla's steel definitely ran strong in their kids. And he was starting to like Addy's older brother. "Ambassador for her own world." He corrected. "But with very strong connections to another one."

"Very strong?" Alex narrowed his eyes. "I was told royal by my father."

"You have been told a lot in the few hours you've been awake."

"I like to keep up to speed. Being asleep for a week means I can go a day or so without it now." Alex pushed at the pillows and ignored Addy's glare.

"Alexandar."

Alex ignored his mother and kept his eyes on Rix, who didn't blink back. He did chuckle though. "My Father's uncle is Nahr Nerilla's life mate. So yes, some would say I am royalty, though it is not through blood." He glanced at Layla. "I never had aspirations to lead my people, and now that I have Addy and Quinn, I am even less inclined. I like travelling and trading and helping my people that way."

"Your crew is all male." Alex eyed Valco and Craith standing by the door.

"And they know I would leave them close to death if they so much as saw a shadowed outline of Addy's form. Touching another's mate is not done."

"Life mates are to be cherished, and females are highly respected with our people." Valco spoke quietly. "Females are less inclined to fight - instead they are ruthless negotiators and rarely start conflict. We respect their wisdom in all situations. Birthing is hard on our females. We cherish the time we get with them and if both mother and child survive, it is highly celebrated." He shuffled, as if not comfortable with everyone's attention focused on him.

"For Rix to have found a mate such as Addy who is clearly a wonderful mother to have saved her child as her friend in such a situation - we would never sabotage that." Craith smirked. "I would ask if you know of six Earth women with similar traits as Addy who wouldn't mind a life travelling space?"

Alex barked out a laugh. "I do not. Not similar to Addy anyway." He chuckled again. "I only mostly know military type women."

Craith nodded. "Maybe Bran would like to meet those females."

"Alex." Addy cut through the chatter and looked down at her brother in his medical-issue sleeping slip before looking imploringly at her mother. "I'm glad you're awake but is everything ok? Where is Dad?"

Layla moved to the other side of Alex's bed and sat. "Alex had just enough oxygen to avoid brain damage, but his body did need some time to recuperate. All the doctors who have seen him – the ones from the battle stations that first saw him; the presidential doctor and those that work for your father – they've all stated he will make a full recovery."

"As for your father … he is currently working with the fallout from the Scraver attack, or more specifically, the gross negligence as a result of ignoring Alex's warning." Layla's voice shook with anger. "All those lives lost." She grasped both Alex and Addy's hands in hers and hung her head in grief.

Rix moved from his spot near Quinn to grasp Addy's shoulder and press a kiss to her hair.

Moving her spare hand, she gripped Rix's hand on her shoulder and gave it a slight squeeze.

"And all the assholes are dead."

"Addy!" Her mother admonished.

"I know it's a horrible thing to think. But they don't have to face the true ramification of their actions. They're dead. And so are thousands of innocent people. Yes, they met a horrible fate due to their actions but it's just...so did so many others." A wave of great sadness hit Addy. All those people she'd worked with and made friends with. Their families would never see those responsible receive punishment from the proper authorities. In a way, they'd skipped it.

"Rix."

Addy and Rix both spun to look at the door when Ralli's voice broke through the tension in the room.

"A small metal-haired woman and many soldiers are on their way down the hall." "That sounds like President Gena and her full legion of guards and aides." Layla stood and moved around the bed to stand near Alex's head. Addy and Rix stood side by side at Alex's hip and faced the door just as President Gena stopped, but didn't enter.

Craith and Valco both moved to fill the doorway from inside.

The President eyed the Farskons. "You certainly are intimidating when you want to be. However, I come in peace and bearing good news." She looked beyond the large wall of muscle at Addy and her family, her gaze landing on Quinn sleeping in the corner. "I'll be quick. Heaven knows you all this time as a family."

Rix growled something low and Craith, Ralli and Valco

backed up a few steps. Gena held up a hand and entered the room alone. Her multitude of an entourage stayed in the hallway.

"Commander Ward. I wanted to tell you personally you have been cleared of all accusations, both ridiculous and those slightly over the top. Ambassador Ward, you too. This entire mess sits squarely on the shoulders of Commander Ward's superiors."

"Good."

Addy snorted at her mother's dry tone. President Gena smiled wryly, before pinning Addy with her grey gaze.

"Next, I never did receive an answer about the senatorial position I offered you at dinner, ambassador."

Glancing at Rix, Addy wrapped her hand around his forearm. She studied the president for a moment then shook her head. "I'd like to politely decline, President Gena." She looked at Quinn pointedly before continuing. "I like my current hours and job requirements. I must think of my family first and then my people. But I would like to continue working on trade deals between the Farskons and the human race."

President Gena grinned. "How convenient that you are now married to the Farskon ambassador. And not at all surprising. However, if at any time in the future you would wish to change your position, all you have to do is message me." Gena gestured to an aide in the hallway. "This is your father's Orb. He won't be far away by the way; however, this Orb now has a direct link to my personal devices. If there is ever anything you think I can help with, please do not hesitate to message me." She glanced at Rix. "I believe that between the two of you, our worlds will have a great future together. Addison, I have a list of my aides and personnel that would like to start fresh, and further their skills by trying some time in space, both short and long term. You can build your team with whoever you like. Handpick the best of my best."

Addy knew her mouth hung open. Stella gave her a shove from the far side of Alex's bed.

"That - that's incredibly generous, President Gena."

"After this mess I think it should just be Gena, please."

"That's incredibly generous, Gena. Wow." Addy didn't know what to say.

"Hardly. After going over the footage in the hallway after the failed trade deal, it was clear we had all the wrong people covering that negotiation - excluding you of course."

The aide Gena had gestured to before politely cleared her throat from the hallway. She held an Orb and seemed unsure as to whether she should hand it to Ralli or to reach past him and Craith to the president. Ralli nodded slightly and held a hand out. The woman smiled shyly before she quickly handed him the Orb avoiding touching him and stepped back the crowd. Ralli snorted but passed the Orb to Craith who gave it to the president.

"Thank you. The list is on this Orb, along with a few other surprises." Gena moved to stand within arm's reach of Addy and Rix. She lowered her voice so only they could hear. "I've also had a live plant of mint quarantined and placed in the bay where your shuttle is docked. For your own studies. I wish to sincerely apologise for the adverse affects it caused."

Valco choked from the other side of the room, thumping a fist to his chest and forcing a few coughs. Addy forced herself not to react while Rix stiffened beside her.

"Thank you, Gena, that's very thoughtful. Luckily the effects were not life-threatening, though more severe than we'd anticipated." She smiled slightly.

"Again, I apologise." Gena stepped back and this time focused on Alex. "Commander. My husband's people are working fast to repair the Earth Cruiser. But they were also nearly finished on a similar model. I'm offering you full command of either if you would like – completely your choice. You can handpick your commanding team and even the passengers you allow on board, from military personnel to space tourist. Essentially I'm offering either Cruiser to you to do with as you will – sanctioned trade missions between planet or leisurely tours of our galaxy."

"Holy shit!" Stella sat down heavily in the chair beside the bed.

Addy stared, astounded at the president's offer, while Layla looked just as shocked.

"Captain of a space cruiser. Alex! Holy shit!" Stella shoved at Alex's shoulder while he simply started at the president like his sister.

Chapter 12

"How the hell could you turn that down?!" Stella hadn't stopped rambling since they'd gotten back to the Farskon ship. She piled her plate high with food and moved down the buffet.

Gorven chuckled as he replaced an empty dish with another piled high with more food.

"You resigned!" Stella added another spoonful. "I mean. A *cruiser*!! And you *resigned*!!" She shook her head and finally fell silent when she spun and pointed at Alex with a long stick of, she didn't know what, but it tasted amazing. She opened her mouth, shook her head again and took a bite of the crunchy covered meat. She huffed again and chewed.

Alex chuckled and didn't answer. He just ate some more. "This food is amazing. No wonder you don't want to leave, Stella." He winked at her and earned another huff.

"Thank you." Gorven smiled at Alex. The elusive Farskon, who mostly stayed close to his kitchen, changed a few other dishes over and took the empty ones back into the kitchen.

Addy smiled. Her family had come back to the Farskon ship a few hours after the president had left Alex's medical suite. Everyone filled the eating area and Gorven had gone above and beyond making sure there was enough food for everyone to eat.

Her parents were on a tour of the ship with Bran and Rix, while Ralli played with Quinn in the corner of the cafeteria. He was currently encouraging Quinn to stand on her own, helping the tot to take steps while holding her hands for support. The males had cleared a small area and placed some toys they had fashioned from spare parts and scraps. Toys that resembled ones they had played with as children, Rix had told her. Layla had teared up when Rix had explained what they were.

Alex had been given strict instructions to take it easy and rest - something he seemed happy enough to do, so long as he was watching or reading something. Or eating. Addy swore that in the last two hours her brother had consumed more in that time then she'd ever seen him eat.

"Careful or all that food will come back up." Valco grinned at Alex across the table they both sat at. Alex just smiled back and ate another bite. Valco raised a brow to which Alex just shrugged.

"Okay, okay. I'll slow down. But this is so easy to eat."

Valco and Addy laughed. She looked up as her parents, Rix and Ralli entered the room. She frowned when she saw their faces.

"What is it?"

"The people repairing the Earth cruiser sent your things over to this ship in an automated delivery pod." Rix answered.

"They've kicked me out of my suite?"

"No, no. It appears they got things confused. The president's husband changed your holdings on your behalf. You've been upgraded to what will be a replica of their suite. A little extra gift from Gena - I presume to mark you as one of the few survivors. The others got upgrades as well, though not as lavish as yours." Her mother smiled and sat down beside Alex while Nolan grinned mysteriously and went straight for the huge piles of food.

"There appears to have been a stowaway in amongst your possessions though, which I think is how things got confused. Seems as though someone hacked the delivery orders and had them sent here instead of to storage until the new suite is completed next week." Layla grinned again and watched the cafeteria doorway.

Pravi entered the cafeteria and laughed at something someone said behind him. A plate clattered to the floor.

"BREE?!"

Stella shot across the room like a laser shot. "What the hell are you doing here?" She hugged her little sister in a tight hold.

"Why else would I sneak onto a foreign spaceship with only a slight rumor telling me that you might be on it?"

Stella leaned back and brushed a lock of fire-red hair that matched her own out of her sister's face. Her expression hardened. "Mother."

"Mother." Bree agreed. They hugged again and Bree buried her face in her sister's hair. "We were told you died with everyone else on the ship. It didn't matter that they couldn't find your body. There were a lot of bodies they couldn't find or identify."

"Shh. I'm ok. We're ok." Stella glanced at Addy before looking back at Bree. A horrible thought struck.

"Oh fuck. Bree, our mother isn't focusing her, ah, efforts on *you*, now is she?" Stella's face paled.

Bree grimaced. "Of course she is. But first, let's sit down. That delivery pod took its sweet time getting over here and I'm starving."

Stella remembered her fallen plate of food and turned back to it, but Gorven appeared from behind the buffet.

"No. Sit with your sibling." He handed her another plate piled high with the same choices she had made on the last one.

She smiled and nodded her thanks and sat at the table next to Alex's table. Bree sat across from her.

Addy moved from her spot and sat next to Bree after giving her a cuddle. Rix and the others got some food and sat around the room.

Everyone was ready to hear Bree's story, except for Ralli, who was still focused on Quinn and her step coaching.

"After you ran away to help Addy – yes, I knew exactly what it was - running away, I think Mother realised she'd pushed you too far by arranging the marriage to that sleazy toy boy of hers. Well, honestly. What the fuck?! Who wouldn't be pushed too far by that? It's disgusting and just well, fucking weird." Bree glanced around the room and grimaced again. "Sorry for the cursing, I'm a bit out of sorts."

"Not all, love. It is fucked up" Layla waved for Bree to continue.

"Well. Yeah, anyways, she kept going along with it with the small hope that you were going to get bored and come back. She really does think we all think like her. Urgh not. But yeah. She also started throwing guys at me. Subtly at first and then the longer you stayed in space, the less and less subtle she got." Bree nodded a smile at Gorven who placed a plate of food in front of her as well. "Then we heard about the Scraver attack. Well 'Mummy Dearest' got hysterical." Bree waved a fork-like utensil at Addy, pale green eyes flashing. "Oh, not in grief. No no. She was pissed that she'd worked so hard on your wedding and then you up and died on her." Bree frowned when Stella laughed.

"Of course she didn't care that her daughter was dead. Oh no. It was the wasted work on my wedding to her brain-dead lover that she was upset about. Pah! Typical Mother."

"Exactly." Bree pointed her fork at Stella. "Yup. So, then she starts working on turning your wedding into your funeral. Dad was furious. Screaming matches ensued. Bad ones. I mean *bad* ones. She was using your death as a publicity stunt." She paused and reached out to hold Stella's hand. "Dad's divorcing her. Apparently, he's just as calculating, actually more so, than as she is. There was a clause in their prenup that specifically stated something about using the death of a child for her gain. He's taking everything. *Everything* Stella. All of it."

"Holy. Fuck." Stella whispered, frozen to the spot.

Layla started to laugh, fits of giggles Addy had never seen her mother in before. "That frigid bitch finally got her comeuppance!" Nolan patted his wife on the back and chuckled with her.

Addy, not all surprised at her mother's opinion of the soon to be Ms Morgan, smirked at Stella.

"But Stella, that's not it." Bree's words stopped the laughter short. "Shit! What else is there?"

"Dad wants you to take over Mother's duties in the company. He sent me to the president's cruiser to so I could find you and make sure you came home to start running the company. You know he planned to retire in a few years anyways."

"Oh god no!" Stella leaned back sharply. "No way. I do NOT do well in board rooms."

"Neither do I." Bree shook her head. "That's why I need you to convince him that Theo is the better choice. Male heir and all that crap."

"Theo? But he's barely twenty?" Nolan looked shocked.

Stella grinned, loving the idea, mostly because she'd had it years ago. She turned to her friend's father. "Yes, twenty-one and he's already completed three different engineering degrees and a master's in computer science. I'm barely equal to a tech assistant compared to Teddy. He might not yet have a head for business but I'm sure Dad can whip that into him in the next few months."

"And Theo will lap it up." Bree nodded. "He's been dying to get a chance to show himself to Dad, but Mother would never allow it. Not her baby boy. No, he needed to have his head in a book at all times."

Stella looked to Rix. He gave a slight nod and smiled at her, knowing where her thinking was going. "Rix offered me a job here, learning the Farskon computer programming styles and languages. I'm sure I can work that into conversation before giving Dad the idea that Theo would be better suited to run the company."

Bree grinned. "Nice! That sounds amazing! It's perfect!" Her smile dimmed. "Is there a chance I can stay out here too?"

"I'm sure between Rix, our new friend the president and Mr and Mrs Ward here, we can think of something. Addy does need to pick her team of trade assistants." She winked.

The sisters fell into quiet chatter as they planned to throw their little brother at their father.

Rix finished his plate and took it to the return then came to sit with Addy. He rested a hand on her knee and pressed a kiss to her dress above where a new mark was hidden. She shuddered and smiled. "Let's-"

"Addy!"

Addy whipped her head around to stare at Ralli. The large male was beaming from ear to pointed ear as he held his arms out around Quinn, but without touching her. Instead, the little girl squealed in delight as she focused on the big male and took a wobbly step unassisted. And then another.

The whole room was silent as everyone watched little Quinn take four steps all on her own.

Addy erupted the moment her daughter fell to her padded bottom. She raced around the table to fall to her knees by her giggling little girl.

"Quinnie! Look at you! My clever little girl!"

Laughing, she helped stand Quinn to her feet and scooted back a little, holding her hands out to catch her if she fell again. "C'mon baby girl. Walk to Mumma!"

Quinn squealed with delight, her little arms out wide for balance. Starring at her mother with her tongue stuck out the corner of her mouth Quinn took another six steps to Addy.

Cheers filled the room.

"Oh my clever little girl! Look at you go!"

᠙

Later Addy smiled down at Quinn's little face as she snuggled into her little pink blanket in her sleep. She was tucked into the same makeshift cot Bran had made for her. Addy was going to keep it, rough crate markings and all until Quinn was too big for it.

"I'm so happy I got to see her first steps in person." She whispered and traced a finger over her daughters' cheek, before closing the doors to her room almost all the way and padding over to the bed where Rix lay.

He smiled at her. "I think the whole crew will have a newfound appreciation for what it is to have a youngling of their own after witnessing those uneven little steps for themselves"

"I think you're right."

Addy drew the bed covered back and lay down. Rix held an arm up and she snuggled into his side, resting her head on his warm shoulder. She lightly trailed her fingers down his torso, over the hard ridges of his stomach.

He breathed in roughly, the arm she was snuggled under curling around to cup her waist.

Addy looked up at him through her lashes and bit her lip.

"You know it's been a little while since we were properly alone." She trailed a finger lower and lower until it disappeared under the covers. She trailed it lower still, grazing the top of his lower hair line. A soft rumble came from Rix's chest and she grinned and kissed the side of his chest.

"You know there's something we haven't tried yet." She rolled on top of her mate and settled herself over his hips. Rix's hands came to rest on the outside of her thighs.

He growled low in his throat again when he realised she wasn't wearing anything under his shirt.

"I do like this view."

His words ended on a groan as Addy moved, slowly rubbing herself on his now rock-hard shaft, her arousal making them both slick. She leant forwards, barely holding herself up as her hands came down on his chest. Gods he felt good.

"Hmm this isn't quite what I had in mind." Collapsing her arms, Addy's mouth found Rix's throat. She gave him a light nip with her teeth and his hips surged up beneath her, making them both groan at the spike of pleasure it caused.

Gritting her teeth, Addy kept kissing her way down Rix's body. Stopping to nip and nibble at his nipple. His low rumbling growls made his body shake and it urged her to continue. She licked at his belly button and still moved lower.

Rix couldn't think. Addy's mouth tormented him as she made her way over his body. His mate wanted to taste every bit on him, it seemed.

Wait. Every bit of him?

He whipped his head up and looked down at Addy as she swirled her tongue through a dip in his abs. She glanced up and her eyes met his. She watched him watch her as her pink tongue licked along his flesh again. She winked at him.

"You taste good." Her soft hand wrapped around his shaft and he jerked. "I bet this tastes better."

Rix was riveted as he watched as Addy's yellow curls fell and block his view. Her warm breath washed over him as her hand started to pump him slowly.

Addy licked her lips. She'd been wanting to try this for days. She pumped him slowly again and leaned even closer. Her tongue touched the head of his cock and she nearly moaned at the taste of him.

He was sweet. She licked at his slit and opened her mouth wide. More of his sweet taste filled her mouth as she took him a little deeper. She moaned around him.

His mate was going to kill him. Rix was sure of it.

He clutched at the bedding and locked his hips down. He didn't want to accidentally thrust up and choke her. His growls froze in his throat as she picked up the pace, her head bobbing up and down, her hand working what her mouth couldn't reach. Every bob took him ever so slightly deeper.

His lungs burned and he suddenly remembered to breathe.

Addy gasped when Rix moved faster than she could track. She found herself flat on her back. One of her feet was thrown over his shoulder while his hand held her other knee wide. Gripping her left hip Rix lined the himself up with her pussy as she panted under him.

"We definitely need to do that more often." She didn't get a chance to reply because she had her breath taken from her when he entered her to the hilt in one smooth stroke.

Rix paused a moment before withdrawing almost all the way and thrusting back in. Addy didn't have a hope of keeping up with his pace as he pounded inside her over and over.

Pressure built and she used her leg to hold herself at the right angle. Rix's cock hit a spot deep inside and she cried out as the climax crashed over her.

Wave after wave of pleasure rippled through her as Rix's movements became jerky, dragging out her orgasm.

Finally, he stilled with a loud snarl. Her inner muscles gripped and milked him as he found his own climax.

They panted together. Slowly Rix moved them without breaking their connection so that they lay together on their sides, her head pillowed on his arm, his chest to her back.

After a while Addy's breathing slowed and he knew she had fallen asleep. Gently he withdrew from her and quietly got up to get a warm cloth to clean them both. When he returned to the bed, he found Addy hadn't moved, but she was watching him with sleepy eyes.

"You care so deeply. I love that about you." She held out a hand to him and he joined her on the bed. He discarded the cloth after gently cleaning her up. As he lay down, Addy rolled to face him.

"I need to tell you something." She studied his face. Her small pale hand resting on his chest.

"Tonight, after dinner, I had Valco check something."

Concern hit Rix in the chest. "Is everything okay?"

Addy smiled gently. "Yes. Everything is fine. Great actually. Like I just said, you're so caring. And the way you are with Quinn makes my insides turn to goo. Which is why I needed to check that something with Valco."

She paused and kissed him lightly. "I'm pregnant, Rix."

Shock tore through him. "What? Say that again?"

Addy laughed softly. "I'm pregnant. It's too early to know when exactly, but I suspect the Mint Mess may have yet another side effect. Super Swimmers." She cupped his face and laughed joyously.

"You're pregnant." Sheer happiness filled Rix. He was going to be a parem! Father! Again! In such a short amount of time.

Rix rolled Addy under him and kissed her. Laughing, she kissed him back. Her hands threaded into his hair and they rolled again. Her soft curls curtained their faces as they smiled at one another.

So many new things were about to happen. But one thing she definitely knew. She was as happy as she could ever be.

Get ready! There's more to come!

Acknowledgements

Sending out a huge thank you to my girlfriends, Ashlee, Aj, Nicole and Caitlin. You're input and pestering me for more chapters is what got this book written. Without your support and total lack of judgement I'd never have finished this.

Also, thank you Michelle, for dotting my i's and crossing my t's. And for also spotting those times my brain simply added a word and my fingers didn't type it.

And finally, a huge thank you to my husband. You barely knew I was even doing this but I knew if I needed your support it was there without question. Thank you for showering the kids or cooking dinner when I was on a roll.

Look Mrs Hume! I've actually done it!

About the Author

A fair, blue-eyed blonde, Megan grew up and lives in the Central Highlands of Queensland. She and her husband are lucky enough to be raising their three crazy children, while also looking forward to many years together.

Megan loves a good cup of tea while catching up with friends and can often be found reading in bed at all hours of the night.

www.ingramcontent.com/pod-product-compliance
Lightning Source LLC
Chambersburg PA
CBHW060430130626
46555CB00005B/2299